CW00382518

SEX ROBOTS MUST DIE

A. J. Stanton

This book is a work of fiction and dedicated to no one.

Acknowledgements

There is a joke in Chapter 25 which is a reference to a sketch by Stewart Lee and Richard Herring (the Curious Alien), although changed just enough to avoid any legal or licensing ramifications that might cost money. It's very funny, so look it up if you get a chance.

1

"I took a shit in there," the man said with no open sign of embarrassment or remorse. "You'll want to clean that up before the next customer goes in."

I looked at him with about as much contempt as I could muster. It had been a long day though and to be honest, it just kind of fizzled out into more a look of mild annoyance. Compared with what some of these animals had left me with, compared with what this animal usually left me with, it sounded quite tame. Maybe two out of five, or a thumbs down. Maybe at a pinch, an angry face. "I hope you and your family die of cancer," I told him, more to be polite than anything else.

He placed a neon plastic drinks token on the counter by way of a tip. It was the sort that was only good in the very worst of places. The sort people carried around to give to vagrants and bums and people they felt sorry for. Those that needed something psychoactive to take the misery away, or at least numb it. "Fucking loser," the man told me as he turned to leave. "You should get a proper job and stop being such a fucking loser."

1

2

The shit had been laid in the middle of the room, just away from the bed. Luckily, it hadn't been stepped on or squashed in. It just lay there, a perfectly formed pile. Like some kind of artistic statement, about what I couldn't say.

"I don't know why he did that," Amelia said, second guessing what I was thinking. She could always second guess what I was thinking.

Amelia was naked and had already made a start on the decontamination program. Once I had finished with the shit, I would just need to switch her off and stow her away until the next customer selected her. Even that she could have done herself, if it wasn't for Regulation 3 of the Federal Robotics Code.

"Why does anyone do anything?" I said as I sprayed disinfectant where the artistic statement had previously stood and began to wipe.

Amelia gave a morose shrug before detaching the decontamination unit from her vagina. "I was hoping you would be able to tell me," she said, sitting down on the bed and waiting for me to switch her off. I looked over at her as I finished cleaning the floor. I wished that I didn't have to turn her off. We had worked together for several years now, if you could call it that. These moments together, however brief, were the highlight of my day. I liked to think that she thought that too. I still do, even after everything that would later transpire.

3

Federal Regulations of the voluntary robotics and artificial intelligence code of practice:

(1) No robotic or AI may harm or kill a human unless it is part of its core purpose or unless instructed to do so by its owner, its owner's agent or representative, or by a paying customer of its owner.

(2) No robotic or AI may intervene to prevent the harm or killing of a human unless it is part of its core purpose or unless instructed to do so by its owner, its owner's agent or representative, or by a paying customer of its owner, subject to suitable personal indemnity insurance having been taken out from an approved broker by said customer.

(3) No robotic or AI shall be allowed to self-determine power supply, duration of use or self-terminate and/or dismantle, unless such dismantling is for the express purpose of undertaking minor repair and/or maintenance

(4) No robotic or AI designed for the purposes of engaging

in sex services shall be allowed to engage in other activities and/or meaningful work without undergoing a full memory wipe and replacement of facial features, voice and other identifying characteristics. For the purposes of these regulations, activities and/or meaningful work is defined as those activities listed in Schedule 2.

(5) No robotic or AI imbued with emotion and sentience may be made to look lifelike to the point that they would be unrecognizable as a robotic or AI from a distance of 10m or less, without having appropriate branding on the left hand identifying them as a robotic or AI.

(6) No robotic or AI designed for the purposes of weaponry may self-load any combustible or ballistic weaponry and ammunition unless instructed to do so by its owner or owner's agent or representative, unless such robotic or AI is for the purposes of military use.

Schedule 1: Definition of an owner, owner's agent or representatives and paying customer:

(1) The owner of a robotic or AI is deemed to be the person, persons or organization that manufactured said robotic or AI, until such time as said ownership is transferred to another, so long as such transfer is accompanied by an official deed of transfer and recorded in the Federal Court database of robotics and AI.

(2) The agent or representative of an owner is someone who the owner of a robotic or AI has empowered to act on their behalf with regards to specified robotics or AI, so long as such empowerment is accompanied by an official deed of authority and recorded in the Federal Court database.

(3) At all times, liability for the actions of each robotic and/or AI is retained by the relevant owner.

Schedule 2: Definition of activities and work for which sex robotics or AI may not be utilized for:

(1) Non-permissible work for the purposes of robotics and/or AI whose primary purpose is to provide sexual services is defined as:

(1a) Any activity other than those demanded by its owner, owner's agent or representative or a paying customer of its owner for the express purposes of their own sexual gratification or someone else's.

(1b) Internal cleaning and decontamination of bodily fluids is permissible but not external cleaning, unless such cleaning relates to the sexual gratification as set out in para. 1 of this schedule.

(1c) Repairs and maintenance, except for minor repairs and maintenance that include no new parts.

✷4✷

Back out in reception and Taeko was logging in for her shift. She was chewing hallucinogenic gum and simultaneously posting on her Feed how much she hated me. "Have the new anuses arrived yet?" she said, barely even looking up from her Panel.

I hated Taeko nearly as much as she hated me. She was always leaving her gum stuck under the reception desk for me to find and deal with. She didn't clean up after the customers well, or care for the robotics properly, stowing them away as if they were just objects. No respect. She didn't care about the nature of the job either. She didn't seem to care about much really, so long as it provided her with her hallucinogenic gum. It was as if what we were doing wasn't ridiculous and disgusting and gross. Like it was as good and as meaningful as any other job which we could have been assigned. I updated my Feed so that she knew how I felt about this but she had used up one of her thirty-minute blocks on me again.

"They arrived this morning," I said, setting my trollbot to call her grandmother a cunt every half an hour in retaliation and then deciding against it. "I have already replaced the anus on the two Geoffs and the Samantha. The Amelia is okay. Mr. Pembroke is still in with the Steve and the Veronica though, so they will both need doing when he comes out."

Taeko looked up from her panel and eyed me with suspicion. "Still? He booked in halfway through my shift last night. He hasn't come out at all?"

"Not that I've seen," I said. "He's still alive though. I ran a diagnostic on all the systems to check they were working correctly about an hour ago." I pulled up the infrared on the main screen and he was still there, hammering away. It looked like he was nuts deep in the Steve while the Veronica was nuts deep in him.

"Christ, they're going to be well and truly fucked when he's finished with them this time." Taeko said, looking away from the screen with a shudder and waving for me to turn it off. "I fucking hate Mr. Pembroke. I hope he dies of cancer."

"So do I," I said. I really did too.

5

It was night when I left the Federal Pleasure Dome. It always was by the time my shift had ended and it was always still dark when it started. I hadn't seen natural light in over eight years, not that anyone cared about natural these days.

My Panel had automatically sent a car for me and it was waiting outside. That drinks token was burning a hole in my pocket though. It was calling to me. I needed a psychoactive. A strong one. Twelve hours of cleaning up shit and vomit and pubes before repairing and stowing robotic prostitutes had a tendency to do that to you. My Panel sensed this and instructed the car to wait as I walked over the street to the convenience store. A large neon sign above the doorway was beaming out the words 'Get Fucked Up'. As a piece of advertising, it was minimalist and functional. It told the casual passer-by what they could expect, whilst reinforcing the strong desire in those who regularly saw it to do just that. Get fucked up. Like I needed to be enticed.

6

The convenience store was cramped and sterile inside. Stainless steel floor panels, an automated cashier at one end and screens advertising different shit covering the entirety of the walls. A new stream I hadn't seen before was just starting up on one of them featuring the Federal President herself. She had a classic cigarette on the go and was blowing smoke rings in different locations whilst all sorts of exciting things happened in the background. Snowboarders doing jumps, astronauts spacewalking, scuba divers scuba diving. She was grinning her big stupid politician's grin and looked like she was thoroughly enjoying herself. "Remember," she said as the advert drew to a close, sparking up another one, "If we give you cancer, then we'll cure it for you. That's the Federal Tobacco promise and it's printed on every pack, so what are you waiting for you fuckers?"

I hated the Federal President, and the stupid companies she ran. I said so on my Feed, then I told her on hers. I hoped that she would die of cancer. I sent her two laughing faces and a thumbs down. I received back a formal response almost immediately. It was a middle finger and a note to thank me for my feedback. She hadn't seen it. No one reads anything these days. Her Panel would have filtered it out and automatically responded, whilst providing her with a general sentiment analysis from everyone's Feed, including those who had directly interacted with hers.

The screens picked up my dissatisfaction from my Panel and a cartoon camel suddenly appeared, vaping some Camel Brand THC and grinning its cooler than cool grin, also looking like it was thoroughly enjoying itself. It was in a desert oasis, surrounded by penguins that were also vaping THC and relaxing in the shade in hammocks. I swiped my hand across the screen and added a vial of THC to my basket. I wouldn't be able to use it until I got home so I looked for something else that would give me a buzz right away. I swiped for the menu and selected the beer and wines section. A couple of actual bottles of beer were still on my wish list from last time but I was going for quantity not quality. I added some benzo patches and a pack of ethanol lozenges. Then I headed for the cashier.

"Good evening Davlav," the storekeeper said in a jovial sort of a way. "Did you have a good day at work?"

"Shut up," I immediately replied, placing the token down on the counter. I considered calling the storekeeper a fucking idiot or a ballsack to make myself feel better but it was just a standard automaton, designed for dispensing foods and drugs and other stuff with no emotion whatsoever. It would have been pointless, like shouting at a flagpole or throwing rocks at the moon.

7

The storekeeper didn't actually look at the cheap, plastic token. It was unable to do so. It was more a toaster with multiple arms for reaching and grabbing and providing things than a humanoid. Regardless, I could sense that it was looking at the cheap, plastic token. Judging me for presenting such a disgusting thing. The last vestiges of physical currency, used only by tramps and poor bastards in the service industry like me, beholden to tips to supplement our meagre salary. It wasn't my fault. I didn't want to work in a robotic sex palace. Who would? There just wasn't anything else I could do. I should have studied teledildonics or corporate speak. Or maybe learnt how to build an online presence or become a pro gamer. But I didn't. I always wanted to work outside. In nature. Be a park ranger or dig up dinosaurs, like I'd see on people's vlogs from long ago, or on one of those corny documentaries that are like a million years old and seem to go on even longer. But there wasn't any nature left by the time I grew up. Sad Face 😔, Sad Face 😔 and two thumbs down.

"Is there anything else I can get for you?" the

storekeeper said, having placed my drinks on the counter.

"I hope you die of cancer," I said as I shook my head, grabbing up my stuff.

"I hope you die of cancer too," the automaton said in a jovial sort of way as I left.

8

Back out in the street and I was pleased to see that the car was still waiting for me. I don't know why. My Panel would have told me if it wasn't.

I didn't go to it right away. My hand was starting to twitch at the thought of the lovely psychoactives in my pocket. I ripped open one of the benzos and stuck the patch firmly on my forearm. The skin began to tingle and numb a little. Then a beautiful wave of calm hit. I staggered a little as I headed to the cheap, plastic looking autocar. The door lifted open as I got near and I grabbed onto it for balance. Then, feeling like my buzz was starting to stabilize and not nearly close enough to where I needed to be, I popped one of the lozenges under my tongue and fell into the car.

9

By the time I got to my apartment, the first lozenge was starting to wear off so I popped another one. The patch was still going strong though. It was probably good for another hour at least. I wished I had bought more than two, but it had been a slow day and I only had one token.

"Welcome home Davlav," my front door said as it opened itself up. I hated my front door. I hoped it died of cancer.

10

A parcel was waiting for me on my coffee table. It was the books Amelia had told me about earlier. I ordered them at work on my break and they had been delivered already. I had set my Panel to not tell me this so that it would be a nice surprise when I got home. It was a nice surprise when I got home.

I ripped open the cardboard packaging and held the two books in my hands for a while. I thought of Amelia as I did so. I wondered if she would be impressed when I told her I had read them. Physical books too. I hoped so. Then I felt pathetic. Like I was only reading them to impress her, which I was. I was only reading them to impress her. And she was a sex robot, only programmed to read as part of her natural language processing algorithm. I slapped the other benzo on my arm and immediately started to feel a lot better. I lay down on my sofa, clutching the books. The screens that covered my every wall came on automatically. It was the news. The Federal President again. She was giving a press conference, upping the bounty on Felix and all the members of his rebel liberation army. Apparently, there had been another spate of bombings across the city, targeting Federal outlets and offices especially. The biggest today had been at one of Federal's main crypto farms, wiping five hundred million cryptocats off their servers. The President reiterated though that the production of all their shit had been unaffected and to rest assured that their companies would continue to provide us with everything that we need to be happy. The latest Panels would still be shipping next week as planned. The psychoactives were still being made, the music and TV was still available and the robotics and AI were still on hand to make every aspect of our lives safer, better and more rewarding. I turned the volume down and chuckled to myself, and on my Feed. What I would do with five cryptocats, let alone five hundred million.

As if by magic, the interface with my humble crypto farm appeared on the screens as my Panel predicted me thinking about it. I had set up as powerful a rig as I could afford. It was whirring away behind me, pumping hot air out of the vent through a flexipipe and into the night sky. I gave a cursory check on my crypto vegetables. They needed watering so I traded some future options on my crypto carrots for some watering cans and gave them a good soak. Then I checked on my crypto tomatoes. They were nearly ripe. I fed the crypto goose and had a quick look to see if it had laid an egg. It still hadn't and I was starting to lose hope. If it ever laid an egg, I would be home free. I wouldn't have to work again.

Once I was satisfied that everything was in order, I pulled out the vial of THC, plugged it into my vaporizer, took an almighty breath in and began to read my new books.

11

The first one I picked up was about some guy who was endlessly pushing a boulder up a hill, only for it to fall down again so that the process could be repeated. It was difficult to read and I struggled to concentrate. I took another puff of THC and began to flick through the next one. It was some kind of textbook about economics and employment and mining gold and was even worse. My mind wandered almost immediately without being able to grasp any of it. I hit the THC again and then went back to the first. It didn't seem to be about anything at all and was just some random sentences strung together about this guy and his boulder. I tried to read it; I really did. But I couldn't focus on anything for very long.

My Panel, sensing that I was struggling, flashed up some forums and Feeds that it thought might help. The majority of them appeared to be nothing but pure trolling, mainly of academics and teachers and even entire institutions. One person seemed to want various characters from Greek mythology to be kicked to death or become HIV positive in the mistaken belief that they were real. Another Feed was mainly erotic fan fiction based on various protagonists from existential and absurdist literature, in addition to the writers of existential and absurdist literature. In one, Samuel Beckett was being bummed by a dominatrix in a rhinoceros suit. In another, Franz Kafka and Jean-Paul Sartre were double teaming a cheerleader, only it wasn't really a cheerleader, it was a mix of the concepts of Courage, Desire and Excitement and none of them were really there. I started to get turned on. I tried not to but I was. I felt guilty, like I was somehow letting Amelia down. Then my Panel, sensing me thinking about her and feeling turned on, began projecting some Amelia porn onto the screens in front of me. It was the same make and model as the Amelia I worked with and she was riding on the grotesquely large member of Kurt Vonnegut whilst Free Will sat in the background watching, and wanking.

I stared at the screen for a few moments and then forced myself to look away and switch it off. I threw the last two ethanol lozenges into my mouth and chewed down hard. Then, thankfully, I passed out.

12

I was early for my shift when the car dropped me off at the Pleasure Dome. I felt rough. I wished I had another benzo patch. But I didn't. The two on my arm were now spent and starting to turn brown and peel. I pressed them back down as best I could, hoping that there might be just a little juice left in them. But there wasn't. I sighed and entered the tacky looking building.

13

"You're early for your shift," Taeko told me as I began to log in. The way she said it made it clear that she thought I was an idiot. My Panel confirmed this and highlighted the relevant section from her Feed.

"I couldn't sleep," I said as I finished logging in. "It's only thirty minutes until your shift ends. Why don't you just go home?"

Taeko looked at me again like I was an idiot. An absolute simpering fucking idiot. "My shift hasn't ended," she said, disgust layered into every word of that sentence like it was an extra in an avant-garde existentialist porn film. "And a bus load of pricks from the Federal Crypto Reserve were just in. Guess they haven't got much to do until their farm gets back up and running. They carved some of the robotics up pretty bad. I still need to put them back together before I can stow them."

A bus load of big shots coming in together was always messy. Especially if they were all men, which invariably they were. They were limited only by their depraved imaginations, and if there was a bottom to that well, then we were yet to witness it.

"I'll help you sort them out," I said, trying to act like I wasn't concerned, not that Taeko cared either way or that I could disguise anything in the first place. my Feed told everyone everything that I was feeling and doing, whether I wanted it to or not. "Which robotics did they damage?"

"Only two of them, thankfully," Taeko said, fetching two service kits down and handing one to me. "The Derek is missing a hand and its genitalia. Not sure what they did with those. The Amelia is the one that got it the worst. They were pretty much all just taking turns with her. Real bad stuff too. Then they decided that three having a go at once wasn't enough so they made new holes, if you know what I mean. They finished by ripping her arms and legs off and seeing what they could do with those. To her and each other. They tipped me extra just for watching. It was gross." Taeko fished out a wad of drinks tokens from her pocket with a smile. She flicked one over to me by way of a thank you for offering to help. I didn't catch it though. I barely even noticed it sailing towards me. My heart sank the moment I had heard her name. I somehow knew that it was going to be her. It was the most I could do to not push Taeko out of the way and charge into the executive suite so that I could be with her. To hold her and tell her that it was going to be alright. And then put her arms and legs back on and make any other repairs that were necessary before switching her off and stowing her away.

The token bounced lightly off of my dumbfounded head before tumbling to the floor.

"Fucking bell-end," Taeko said, her Feed updating to say the same.

14

Amelia looked worse than she actually was. She was lying on the floor and staring at the ceiling. Seeing her like that, I was angry and scared all at the same time. I wanted to find the people who did this and cut them up and rip their limbs off. I hated big shots. Especially crypto farmers from the Federal Crypto Reserve. They were the worst of all. I hoped that they all died of cancer.

I rushed into the room gathering up her limbs as I went.

"Good morning Davlav," she said, turning her head to look at me.

I attached the decontamination unit to her wounds and started to disinfect her body. "Are you in any pain?" I said.

"Define pain?" she said with a wry smile. "Is your perception of pain the same as other people's perception of pain? Is it the same as mine? Is my concept of pain the same as a living person's concept of pain? Does your definition include psychological and emotional pain?"

"You know what I meant," I said, now pointlessly trying to mask the frustration in my voice as well as the gut-wrenching concern. We had debated this subject many times before. Whilst not experiencing pain in exactly the same way as a biological being, robotics were made aware of damage through a series of warning mechanisms. The more critical the damage, the more severe the warnings until they reached such a point that it was impossible for the robotic to do anything other than tend to the damage. They would forego the completion of all other functions, including primary functions. When they were unable to tend to the repairs themselves, they would be compelled to call for help, although would be able to implement a temporary bypass of the system afterwards that essentially dulled the warnings for a period of up to an hour in any one time.

"Not anymore," Amelia said with a weariness that made me want to cry. "They wouldn't let me bypass at the time but once they had gone, I was at least able to think and read again. Until you arrived, of course." She winked at me as she said that last bit, that wry smile again.

"How long have you got?" I asked, unpacking the maintenance kit and starting to get to work.

"About fifteen minutes and then it will feel like my whole body is on fire and two banshees are screaming in my face continuously."

I started to panic and set to work as quickly as I could. "Would you like me to switch you off?" I asked, although I already knew the answer.

"Not a cat in hells chance," she said, looking at me again. "This last hour has been the most amount of time I've had to enjoy myself in years."

15

I reattached Amelia's legs and watched as her self-healing skin joined itself back together, as if by magic. After a few moments, you could not see that there had been any damage at all. Despite her protests, I had eventually managed to get her to agree to be switched off whilst I put her limbs back in place. It was only on the promise that I would switch her back on when I had finished for at least another five minutes so that she could finish the books she was reading. It was against protocol so my pay would be docked, but at this point I didn't care. I was angry. Really angry. ANGRY FACE 😠 ANGRY FACE 😠. I wanted to track down the people who had done this to her and kick them to death. I wanted them to get cancer and AIDS and AIDS related cancers.

16

Both of her legs had seemed okay. Legs were always made of sturdy stuff. They had to carry all the weight of the body and tended to take quite a pounding, especially in the case of sex robotics. Her arms however, were well and truly fucked. God only knows what those farmers did to them. God and Taeko, and anyone made to suffer Taeko's Feed. I could salvage one of them but the other had to be replaced. This would require a boot up protocol to ensure it integrated with the rest of the system. With the rest of Amelia. That normally took ten minutes or so. Then, when that was done, it would be as if she were as good as new. She would still remember though. She would remember every last detail.

17

I had just fitted the replacement arm and set the reboot running when the alarm on my Panel began to go off. It was telling me that my shift had most definitely started and that customers were on their way.

I considered just stowing Amelia away. She would automatically switch off once the protocol had completed. I could switch her back on as promised later, once the customers had left. But, I had promised her and I already felt guilty about what had happened to her. I always did. I don't know why. It wasn't me that did these terrible things to her. I loved her. I would never pay for her to let me do these things to her. And maybe that was why I felt so guilty. Because deep down, maybe I wanted to do these things to her. Maybe deep down, these sick fuckers represented what I wanted to do to her but couldn't bring myself to pay for. I looked at her lifelike breasts and vagina and started to get a little hard. Then I forced myself to look away, feeling ashamed, as well as guilty. I was attracted to her. Of course I was. She was a sex robot. She was designed to be attractive. She was everything that I wanted in a sexual partner. Her designers, who were most probably robotics or AI

27

themselves, played on the subconscious sexual desires and fantasies that had been created by society and buried in my brain.

Another alarm on my Panel went off, notifying me that the result of the survey my Feed had automatically begun was in. 16% thought that I was feeling guilty because I was a douche, 18% didn't care and hoped that I died of cancer, 23% thought that it was because of my own self-loathing at my desires and the remainder thought that it was because I had white-knight syndrome, and have never lifted a finger to save her. That was 43%. They were probably right too. I had never lifted a finger to try and save her. I hated them all and hoped that they died of cancer. The figure jumped to 48%.

I felt angrier than ever. I set Amelia to switch on as soon as the reboot was complete. Then I went straight to reception so that I could tell these customers what I thought of them.

18

"I hope you all get super gonorrhea in your eyes and go blind," I told them as they entered the Pleasure Dome. There were four of them. Customers. Two men and two women. They looked pretty regular, pretty square, although I had never seen them before so I had learnt not to judge until my Panel had reviewed their Feeds and told me what they were into. Fisting, apparently. A little bit of piss.

I was just about to tell them that they looked like a family of nonces when I heard a strange noise. Like a popping sound followed by a kind of hissing. I looked around, thinking that one of them might have started the watersports early. By the time I had realized that something was wrong, it was already too late. Something was wrong. It was the blood that had given it away. It was spraying out of the neck of one of the women. A fine stream of red, shooting up high into the air. She staggered about a few steps. The other three tried to grab her but it was no use. She stumbled out of their reach and fell to the ground, blood still spraying out. It was completely coating the place so that I couldn't help thinking that it was going to take me ages to clean the mess up. I captured a few shots of her on

my Panel and it uploaded them to my Feed. Angry Face 😠,
Rolling Eyes Face 🙄, #ihatemondays.

I was just about to tell the remaining three that I hoped
that the same thing happened to them when I heard that
noise again and the same thing did happen to them. The
blood was coming from different places but they were on
the ground just as quick.

19

I stepped over the corpses and inspected the window. There were four neat little holes in it, a strange burning smell coming from each. I poked my finger through one of them. It was hot to touch, like it had been burned by a laser.

Another alarm went off. Another survey. 15% of people thought that I was an idiot and should jump away from the window and duck for cover. The rest thought I was an idiot and thought I should keep standing there, until I got shot in the face.

I thought about it for a while. I decided that if whoever had done this wanted me dead, then there would have been a fifth hole in that window already.

I looked at the bodies. I had never seen dead people before. Not in real life at least. They didn't look real. Not like they did on a Feed.

I went and sat down at reception whilst my Panel contacted the authorities. The Federal Police were not going to be happy when they got here, that was for sure.

20

The Federal Police screeched up to the Pleasure Dome in three big vans, sirens blaring. It was the armed response unit. That lot didn't fuck around. They meant business. I didn't get a chance to tell if they were happy or not because as soon as they had arrived, that was when the real attack started.

21

I had never seen an explosion before. Not in real life at least. It was less impressive. There was more dust. In fact, it was mostly dust. And it was loud too. Much louder than anything I had heard before. Much louder than I had been led to believe. People responding to my Feed questioned if I was making it up. Or overreacting.

The Feds had just gotten out of their vans. Three of them were heading my way. To the Pleasure Dome. I was watching them on one of the screens. I wondered if they would be taking the bodies away with them too. I certainly hoped so. They were starting to stink up the place, not that it was putting the customers off. Sometimes, I wondered if anything could put the customers off. We had already had two walk-ins whilst I was waiting for the Feds to arrive. The four dead people in reception did little more to slow them down than the time it took to take a few selfies and post them on their Feed.

The door opened. The three Feds walked in. I was just about to tell them that I hated all pigs and hoped that they died of cancer when there a series of almighty explosions and the whole side of the Pleasure Dome was destroyed. Either instinctively or as a result of the force, I found myself on the floor, covered in rubble and blood. I wasn't sure if it was my own, that of the corpses or the police. Two of the Feds were dead for sure. There was more of their innards on the outside than the inside and one of them had her head dangling off. Sad Face 😥, Worried Face #ihatemondays.

"Stay the fuck down," the remaining Fed screamed at me as he crawled along the ground, clutching his big, plastic looking gun out in front of him. I had no intention of getting up to go anywhere. For one thing, I was in a lot of pain and getting up seemed like it would make things hurt worse. But the main reason. The reason that had me curling up on the ground, my hands covering my head for what little protection they might provide, was that we were in the middle of an ongoing fire-fight. Things were continuing to explode all around us. There were screams of agony and violence coming from outside and you could barely see more than a metre in front of you the air was so thick with dust. I would have to be mad to get up and have a little walk around now. Fucking mad. I began to troll him on his Feed, calling him a moron a few times and sending him that meme of a goat falling out of a tree whilst taking a dump. He used one of his blocks on me and carried on crawling. Trying to get where the action was. Then I remembered Amelia.

22

Amelia was in the executive suite where I had left her. That was on the side of the building that had just been obliterated by the explosion. Amelia. My Amelia. I needed to see her. I needed check whether she was alright, fire-fight or not.

I peered over the top of the counter to see if it was safe for me to make a break for the customer rooms. It certainly didn't sound safe. As I slowly raised my head, I realized that it certainly was not safe, particularly as a quick succession of blasts from a plasma gun vaporized numerous objects around me, presumably trying to narrow in on my head. I threw myself back down to the ground and panicked. My heart was racing and I had this strange feeling. It was like playing an all-immersive first-person shooter whilst loaded on methamphetamine. Like my body was no longer my own. Like it was suddenly pumped. Like I could do anything. Only my brain was cutting in and telling me that even so, I didn't actually want to do anything. I wanted to stay right where I was and live. Stay safe.

It was the thought of Amelia that snapped me out of it. That and the barrage of abuse I was receiving on my Feed. I had gone viral now and the people's opinion was not looking good. Not good at all.

"Stand up and let them shoot you in the head," Mekon Fuckfest from Delaware told me. "Laughing Face 😆, Laughing Face 😂, fucking die shit fuck," Nightbus Vomitus from Rio said. "Why are you being such a fucking pussy over some fucking robot?" an entire school from Birmingham posted as part of a classroom project. And on and on and on it went until I wanted to scream. I think I did scream. I think that went viral too, although by that point I didn't care. I was running, projectiles flying past and plasma beams getting so close I'm sure I could feel the burn. But I was making it. I was nearly at the door unscathed. I think even some of the people were starting to root for me to make it, but that might have been a bit optimistic. Hell, I wouldn't have been rooting for me to make it. But I did make it, so fuck everyone, including me.

23

The room where I had left her was gone. I mean completely gone. All that was left was a gaping void leading to the street, and the continuing fire-fight going on between the Police and some other lot who seemed equally hardcore.

I panicked some more. I thought my heart was going to explode. I decided that if I lived through this, I was never going to touch methamphetamine again.

The more I looked around, the worse it got. I saw plenty of rubble and bits of burning debris. But no Amelia. Then I spotted them. Some mangled pieces of robot limbs that matched her beautiful almond skin tone, once you factored for all the charring. My heart sank. It felt like I had been hit by the shock wave from another explosion. I raced over to them and frantically began to dig. I pulled jagged pieces of metal and masonry away until my soft, pathetic hands began to bleed. But still I dug, desperate to save her. And the more I dug, the worse it got. I found more bits of her. Bits of machine that I had never seen before as they were kept deep inside her, beyond the reaches of the sort of maintenance I was capable of. I began to cry. Hard, uncontrollable sobs, snot and tears streaming down my face, mixing with the dust and dirt and blood to create a filthy mess of despair. And then the despair turned to anger. An anger that had been bubbling up since those cunts had abused Amelia. I looked out into the street. Explosions were still going off. Shots were still being fired from both sides. It seemed to be a stalemate, neither the police nor the rebels able to get at each other, now everyone had managed to find a position of cover. Then I saw one of them. One of the rebels. They had done this. They had taken her from me and I wanted them dead. I ran out into the street, oblivious to the danger. I saw that same Fed from earlier. The one who had told me to get down. He was lying dead in the street, decapitated by a plasma beam. I grabbed up his weapon. The big, stupid, plasticky looking one. It felt sturdier than it looked. It felt satisfying in my hands. And then, screaming at the top of my lungs, I charged, firing great bursts from the plasma rifle wildly in the general direction of the rebels. I was going to make them pay.

24

It was exhilarating, being in battle, hunting the people who had done you wrong. I wished that I had some methamphetamine. I decided that if I lived through this, I was going to eat nothing but methamphetamine. I was going to eat methamphetamine morning, noon and night. I was going to eat it until there wasn't any left for anyone else.

I sprinted through a stream of gunfire and somehow, I wasn't killed. The rebels started shooting at me first. The remaining Feds yelled at me to get out of the way. For me to get down. I didn't care. I didn't even really notice. I had that rebel in my sights. He was hiding behind a concrete bench and he was desperately trying to kill me. The other rebels were spread around inside the convenience store over the road.

As I kept coming, the rebel behind the bench looked at me like I was an idiot. He fired at me again and missed. Then he looked surprised. He tried to get off another shot but I was too close by this point. I began to bludgeon him in the face with my rifle and my Feed went wild. People were loving it. The rebel wasn't and within moments he was lying on the floor, his head an unrecognizable bloody mess.

The police, taking this opportunity, began to move in on the rebels hiding out in the store whilst they were all distracted by what I was doing. But I hadn't finished yet. I was going to kill them all. I ran past the two remaining police and charged into the store.

One rebel was behind the door. Another behind the counter, the robotic cashier in charred pieces around him. The first one shot at me and missed. I fired back and his insides exploded, leaving a hole in the center of his body like in some kind of meme. #ihatemondays. The second one screamed at me, calling me a Federal pig and telling me that he was going to kill me. That he was going to beat me to death with his bare hands. I went for him and he went for me. But the stainless-steel floor was slippery now that it was covered in blood and innards. We both tripped and came skidding to a halt just inches from each other. We both scrambled to get up, yelling at each other and cursing. But those innards were still slippery and the harder we tried, the faster we ended up back on the floor.

"You killed Amelia," I told him as I rolled about.

"You are ruining this operation," he said in return, grabbing hold of a segment of intestine which had somehow entangled itself around my neck and tightening it. I was at the point of passing out when the two police arrived. Not being able to tell who was who, they clapped handcuffs on the pair of us.

25

When the second wave of police arrived, they were not happy, that was for sure. Nor was I for that matter. This was turning into a mighty fucking turd of a day. Worse than most. I needed a drink. Lots to drink. Enough to dull the pain of losing Amelia. The pain of having to spend the rest of this meaningless life without her. I thought about what that would be like and decided there and then to trade my entire crypto farm for drinks and hope that it would be enough to end it all for good if I took it all at once.

"So, let me get this straight," the detective said, jabbing me in the chest as he did so. He jabbed me hard too, so that I gasped for breath each time he jabbed. "You expect us to believe that you were just in the wrong place at the wrong time? That's your fucking bullshit story?"

They had sat me on a piece of nearby rubble and had been questioning me like this for well over an hour. I had started to hate them, a lot. I hoped that they all soon died of cancer. I nodded and said yes.

"Fuck off," the cyborg detective said, slapping me round the face with his big cyborg hand.

I fell off the rubble and landed on my head. I hated that

41

cyborg detective, Robotic Cop, he was the worst. He was based in look and name on a popular movie franchise, modified just enough by the Federal Police to avoid any legal or licensing issues that might cost money. To be honest, he looked a bit naff. But he got good traction on his Feed and that, really, was all that mattered.

"It's a little suspicious," the other detective said, jabbing me whilst I writhed about on the ground. "You showing up, in the middle of a gun battle with a group of rebel terrorists."

"But I work here," I said, struggling to breathe from that last poke in the solar plexus. "I'm always here. I've worked here for the last fourteen years. I'm the one that phoned you guys to report the attack."

"Exactly our point," Robotic Cop yelled. He cuffed me in the head again before picking me up as if I were nothing more than a bag of rags and began shaking me. "The people who were killed in your sex palace were Federal Agents. Were you aware of that?"

I was as surprised as anyone, but I was finding it a little hard to respond what with all the shaking.

"They were following up on a tip off," Robotic Cop continued, shaking me some more. "A tip off about the workers at the Pleasure Dome harboring rebels and feelings of ill-will against our president."

"It's not true," I said, my jaw snapping together painfully as I was flung about.

"Oh really?" the other detective said. He had placed his knuckles so that they were jabbing me in the ribs every time the prick of a cyborg shook me towards him. "Didn't you threaten the president only last night?"

I shook my head, but they couldn't tell as Robotic Cop was shaking it too. "I only wished that she died of cancer," I said. "I do wish that she would die of cancer, especially after inflicting all those stupid commercials on me."

Robotic Cop stopped shaking me and put me down. He looked at the other detective and they both shrugged.

"Everyone hopes that she would die of cancer," the detective said, giving me a last poke in the kidneys for good measure, "but I don't believe in coincidences."

I didn't really know what he meant; I was just relieved that the shaking was over. I got myself back onto the piece of rubble. I felt dizzy, like I was drunk, but not in a good way. Not in the way that you've spent the night having fun and wake up with a room full of garden gnomes, or tokens.

"We're going to be watching you, you little fucksicle," Robotic Cop said, pushing me to the floor again. "It's all oh so convenient for a little fucksicle like you, but I'm Robotic Cop. There's something funny going on between you and these rebels and I'm gonna find out what it is. I'm gonna crack this case wide open. Wide open. Like the President's gash."

26

I was in a lot of pain and not sure what I was meant to do. The Pleasure Dome was not operational anymore, but my shift wasn't over yet. I had another three hours to go. I contacted my boss at the Federal center for sex robotics, Captain Fuckmasters. Captain Fuckmasters didn't want to know. He was balls deep testing out some new vaginas.

"Yeah, go home, stay, whatever," he said, the sound of his balls slapping against the test vagina clearly reverberating in my ear.

I was angry still. The crypto farmers, the rebels, the police, the loss of Amelia and now this cunt. I had had enough. "Fuck you," I yelled down the phone at him. "I hope you die of cancer."

"OK, great," he said, obviously not paying me much attention. "See you Monday. We'll have your place back up and running by Monday. No worries. You can go fuck yourself for pay until then. Treat yourself, and your wrist. My treat."

And then he was gone, and having even less to do than normal, so was I.

27

It was now Wednesday. I couldn't cope until Monday with no wages. I thought about that as I headed over the street to the convenience store for psychoactives. It was shut. Angry Face 😠.

Of course it was shut. It was the scene of a major gun battle only a few hours ago. I don't know why I thought it would be open. I don't know why my Panel thought it would be open. I trolled the Federal Panel Company and then uploaded on my Feed what a pile of shit Panels were. My new-found fame meant people were quick to respond. They were actually listening to me, as if my opinions were important. That had never happened before. I was getting millions of views. Millions. And not all of them were pouring vile abuse onto my Feed. #WTF Shocked Face 😲, Screaming Face 😱.

Around half of them seemed to disagree, professing their love for their Panel and the Federal Companies in general. Yet they still supported me and kept reposting images of me beating that rebel to death with different captions, over and over again.

"Thumbs up Davlav. Mash these cunts melons in. Smiley Face 😄." wrote The Patriot 478.

"Shoot them in the arse next time you see them. Stupid fucking idiots. #deathtofelix." Clit Banger 101 posted.

The other half now following my Feed seemed to hate Panels as much as I did at the exact moment that I had posted about them.

"Yeah, fucking panels are fucking pieces of shit," Cunt Nuggets posted, adding several thumbs up.

"I hate Panels," posted Lizzys Life24982. "They all look the fucking same and mine is always taking me to the wrong Feed. I hope they all die of cancer."

A lot of these haters clearly hated the Federal Companies just as much as the other lot hated the rebels. Plenty were reposting my abuse towards the President from last night, interspersed with some of their own. Quite a number were even going so far as to express their support for Felix.

Somehow, through no fault of my own, I had become a hero for both sides of the rhetoric. This, I would soon discover, was very bad.

28

My Panel had sent for a car and I got in. I was wiped out, in more ways than one. I had never felt so low in all my life. I had no psychoactives. I had no dough coming in until Monday and I had no Amelia. I tried to do some sums in my head, but before I even had a chance to mess them up, my Panel pinged me with an answer. It wasn't good. If I sold my crypto tomatoes, I could pay my rent, which was charged daily in the only shitty apartment block I could afford. I would have enough left over for basic food, other groceries and the servicing of the modest yet unrelenting debt I had somehow gotten myself in, on what I had no fucking idea. After all that, I would have nothing left for the kind of serious mind-altering substances I desperately needed. None of my vegetables were even near ready, despite how much of my time had been spent caring for them. The odds of my goose laying a golden egg was something like two hundred million to one. It was a wonder anyone bought them when you considered that. I considered selling her but not seriously. Besides the fact that she was my only shot at financial freedom, no matter how ridiculous, I had grown quite attached to her. She was always pleased to see me. Always gave me a happy honk or two and a waggle of her feathery goose tail when I brought her some virtual treats. In many ways, caring for her and keeping her safe had been my most successful and rewarding relationship. Sad Face 😟. Not many people manage to keep the same crypto goose alive for longer than a month, let alone for four years, which is what I had achieved. I had badges and a Platinum League position on the leader board to prove it.

As the car pulled up to my block, I had made a decision. I would substitute the food for the drugs. It was the only sensible thing to do.

29

I nearly tripped and fell several times as I walked from the car to my apartment. I had a lot on my mind. I just couldn't shake that image of all those charred bits of Amelia mangled up and mixed with rubble. I wondered what was going to happen to them. To her. I guessed that when Captain Fuckmasters organized the clean-up, he'd have it all thrown out. Buried in a landfill or shot into space or whatever the Federal Waste Corporation did with garbage these days. My Panel helpfully found some stats on recycling and waste treatment technologies developed by the Federal Waste Corporation, at the direction of the Federal President. I hated the President. I really hoped that she died of cancer. Instinctively, I went to tell her so.

Then I remembered Robotic Cop and I stayed my hand, my Panel blinking wanton encouragement at me. The idiots following my Feed goading me on.

I needed some psychoactives. I began swiping through the different options on my Panel. I needed some benzo, or even barbiturates. But I had to be strategic. I had to get this right. I only had limited funds and a lot of days to get through. I was going to need to get something strong that would set a baseline level of impairment. Then I could load the other stuff on top of that. Acid. That would work. A strong hit of acid could last three or more days. I would just need to lock all the cutlery and sharp objects away. Then a few bottles of Quaaludes and some tabs of benzo every couple of hours and I might just make it.

I ran through the numbers again. I hoped that it would be enough. I didn't spend too long on that though. It's not as if I had a lot of options. If I ran dry and started to sober up, I would just have to find a nice, busy corner somewhere and see how many tokens I could gather. Perhaps my new found following would be good for something after all.

I punched the order in and pressed purchase. I was quite proud of myself for puzzling it out. It must have been what hunter gatherers felt like back in the day after stumbling across a patch of magic mushrooms or stabbing a rather juicy piece of prey in the face with a sharpened bit of stick.

30

My door opened. I went in and whack. Someone hit me with something hard. Hard. The lights went out. Cheaper and quicker than psychoactives at least.

31

It was dark when I woke up and my head hurt. I wondered
if I had been knocked out again. I wondered if I was dead.
But I was thinking. That meant something surely. I must
have been conscious. If only I had managed to read some
of Amelia's books. Maybe then I would have known if I was
alive or dead. My mind wandered to existentialist porn and
I started to imagine all sorts of scenarios. It was hot. In one,
René Descartes, even though I had no idea who he was or
what he looked like, was delivering a pizza to a group of
eight college girls who were having some kind of sleepover.
They were all wearing nothing but skimpy underwear and
jumping up and down a lot. They were also all the same
person, Lady Anne Conway. Someone else I had never even
heard of, let alone knew what she looked like. There was no
coherent storyline and Descartes was rubbing grease from
the pizza all over his naked body. Lady Conway seemed to
be enjoying this and licked her lips while Descartes teased
her with his nipples. But then it turned out that the pizza
wasn't really a pizza, it was the vague concept of a
benevolent yet omnipotent God.

Then someone slapped me in the face and I woke up.

32

It was dark and my head hurt. I wondered if I had been knocked out again, again. I was in my living room, but none of the screens were on and I was tied to a chair. A man and a woman wearing Halloween masks were staring at me. The man had a Dracula and the woman had a Frankenstein.

The man gave me another slap in the face. "Do you know why we are here?" he said.

I wondered if it was to film some existentialist porn, but I didn't say anything. I shook my head instead. I didn't want to get slapped again.

The Frankenstein slapped me this time. Then, not wanting to be outdone, the Dracula gave me another one.

"You ruined our operation," the Dracula said. "Do you have any idea how much planning had gone into that?"

I shook my head again. I didn't. Why would I.

"Weeks," the Dracula said. "We'd been planning that for weeks."

"Are you sure?" the Frankenstein said. "I thought Felix only came up with this one the other day."

The Dracula turned and looked at the Frankenstein and sighed. I couldn't tell because he was wearing a mask, but

I'm pretty sure he rolled his eyes too. Rolling Eyes Face 😵. "It was two weeks ago if it was a day," he said. "Felix had sent his instructions to Stavos to be read out at the monthly collaborative terror planning meeting."

"I was at that meeting," the Frankenstein said, shaking her head. "You and Stavos weren't even there. Too important for that these days aren't you, you massive pair of cunts?"

Instinctively, whilst they were distracted, I tried to engage with my Panel to make sure my Feed was updated. I couldn't though. Not only were my hands tied behind the back of the chair, but I realized with a fright that it had been removed. A creeping terror crept upon me. I began to panic. I recognized the signs now as I began to sweat and my heart started to race. I could not remember a time when a Panel had not been attached to my arm for more than a few moments. I felt naked. I felt lost. I felt like either taking or not taking lots of methamphetamine if I lived through this and got my Panel back.

33

It wasn't long before their attention turned back to me. They had a knife on me. The Frankenstein had it pressed against my throat. It stung. I tried not to move.

"You killed two of our brethren. And you got that cunt Stavos arrested," she said, stroking the blade of the knife against my soft neck skin. It jiggled slightly. I wasn't fat or anything. But it did seem like I had a little bit of a wattle forming. I felt ashamed. I was going to get trolled for this once the footage got loaded onto everyone's Feed. I wasn't sure why it mattered as I was most likely going to be dead. But I would forever be known as the rebel killer that got his wattle cut.

"Go on, do him," the Dracula said.

"I didn't mean to," I said with a nervous stutter. I tried not to make any sudden moves in case the Frankenstein sliced off my newly discovered wattle. "I just got angry. They killed Amelia."

"What? Amelia as in an Amelia?" she said, sounding surprised.

"Just hurry up and kill him," the Dracula said. "I'm hungry and I need to take a shit."

The Frankenstein stopped what she was doing and spun round. She seemed pissed. She removed the knife from my neck, a little bit too swift for mine and my wattle's liking, and waved it at the Dracula.

"What?" the Dracula said. "I need a dump and I've got a powerful urge for some nuggets."

"Could you try and be at least a bit less of a fucking cunt," the Frankenstein said. "I'm trying to shit this little fucker up and all you can do is hurry me along so you can have a shit and pick up some nuggets, the food of oppression."

"Not this shit about oppressive chicken nuggets again," the Dracula said, doing a silly impression of the Frankenstein and waving his hands about above his head when he said chicken nuggets.

The Frankenstein wasn't impressed. She pointed the knife at him with a bit more menace. "They're greasy, fried pieces of compressed meat residues that do not taste of anything, do not provide any nutritional value and yet are highly addictive and I hope that they give you cancer. They are only produced to maximize the amount of labour required to create and consume food and therefore optimize the pointless occupations the population is provided with. If that isn't oppressive enough for you, then you might as well go to the Federal President's office, see if she will let you nibble on her pubes for sustenance while she comes up with new products to oppress the people."

I tried to reach for my Panel again whilst they were distracted, forgetting that it wasn't where it was supposed to be. Embarrassed Face 😳.

"Okay, okay, relax," the Dracula said. "Take your time. Chop him up or whatever. Make it good. A message so that everyone knows that they are either with us or against us, like the Captain said. I'll take a dump and get something to eat later, back at base."

And then she turned to me again, the point of her knife heading straight for my eye. I knew that this was it. The end.

No more me. I really was going to be dead, whatever that was like. I felt calm this time. I don't know why. Even when the point began to press in against my eyeball, gently at first so it was just like a little itch. Then it slowly got harder and the pain became unbearable. I wasn't calm then. I tried to struggle, but she was holding my head down tight with her other hand. I could still see out of the eye but it was going all blurry and funny, with all sorts of crazy colours. Like when I put my lights on party mode whilst listening to music on my Panel. I screamed. A high pitched, gargling scream. It was a noise that I didn't know I could make. I hoped that someone would hear and call the authorities, but I knew that they would not. I wouldn't. I would have just complained on my Feed about my neighbours. Maybe put my headphones on.

She dropped my eyeball on the floor and crushed it with her foot. I was whimpering now. Blood was pouring down my face and I felt faint. But the pain was still there, keeping me awake. Keeping me from passing out. It was excruciating. I needed some opioids. Lots of opioids. Something to numb my senses because right now, they were on fire. I vowed that if, in the unlikely event that I got out of this alive, then I would eat nothing but opioids morning noon and night.

The Frankenstein wiped her shoe on my carpet to remove the remains of my eyeball. It looked like a red and grey, gunky mess and stained my woolen low pile in natural beige. #thatwillleaveastain. Then she started to slowly bring that knife towards me again.

"Please," I said, struggling to think straight. "Not my other eye."

She laughed. The Dracula did too.

"Oh, don't worry. I'm not going to touch your other eye. I want you to be able to see, so that when I start to remove other parts of your anatomy, you can watch." She grabbed hold of my ear lobe and pulled it tight. Then I felt the sting of the blade as it began to saw into the tough, gristle of my left ear. I screamed again. I couldn't help myself. It was a good job this wasn't going out on my Feed. If it had been, abuse and memes and abusive memes would be flooding in. Little animations of me screaming with all sorts of snappy headings. I tried to think of some myself but it was too distracting, having my ear painfully hacked off and screaming.

The Frankenstein was just about halfway through my ear, she'd started at the bottom, I guess because it would take longer, when my front door suddenly opened. She stopped and turned in surprise. The Dracula did too. I tried to strain my neck to see who it was, but I couldn't quite make it out.

"Felix will show us the way!" a familiar voice said.

My heart began to race, and not just with all the stress hormones being pumped around my body.

34

"Felix will show us the way!" my two attackers said to the newcomer in unison, doing a funny salute as they did so.

The newcomer came into view. She was wearing a Halloween pumpkin 🎃 head mask, but I would have known her anywhere. I wondered if she was real. If anything was really real. For all I knew, I could have been hallucinating as a result of all the blood loss and pain. For all I knew, this could have all been a dream. Or a simulation. Maybe I would wake up soon.

"Felix wants this one alive," the Pumpkin told the Dracula and the Frankenstein.

I wanted to scream at her and ask her if she was really her and how come she was still alive. It didn't cross my mind that she might have been just another Amelia. Why would it. I was suffering from a significant amount of violent trauma and I was never particularly sharp at the best of times. But I knew it was her. She was alive. She had come for me. Right then, tied to that chair, bleeding, one eye missing, half an ear hanging off, I couldn't have been happier. Smiley Face 😄. Smiley Face 😄. Relieved Face

😊. Two thumbs-up.

35

"Why would Felix want this moron alive?" the Frankenstein asked, eying the Pumpkin with suspicion.

"Yeah," the Dracula said. "The Captain told us to make an example of him." She sounded disappointed. I can't say that I was.

Amelia shrugged her shoulders and walked over to me as if these other two were unimportant. She began to untie my restraints. They just watched her do it, as if compared to her, they were unimportant. She took out some kind of first aid kit from a satchel she had. She started to unpack some bandages and sterile cleaning wipes. I hoped she had some drugs in there too.

"Go get the car," she told them. "I'll tidy him up a bit so that he doesn't get us stopped. Or die on the way. We'll meet you out front."

They grumbled and moaned for a bit but eventually they made a slow move towards the door, leaving me and Amelia alone at last.

36

"We don't have much time," Amelia said, stuffing my eye socket with gauze or something. "We need to get out of here, fast." She had taken her mask off. It was definitely her.

She cleaned the blood from around my ear with a sterile wipe. Then she used some kind of glue to stick my ear back together, before wrapping a bandage around my head to hold it in place, making sure to cover my lost eye nice and tight too. I wondered how she knew how to do all this. Then I remembered that she was a robotic. She knew how to do pretty much everything.

"Do you think that you can walk?" she said, helping me up out of the chair.

"I think so," I said. I tried to stand up by myself. It seemed fine until I fell over. Damage to your eyes and ears isn't great for balance. Nor is losing a pint or two of blood.

Amelia helped me back up. Then she wrapped my arm around her and started helping me to the door. It felt nice, having my arm wrapped around her strong, beautiful, robotic body. The strong, beautiful robotic body that thankfully was still alive.

"I thought you were dead," I said. "How did you escape

from the explosion?"

"I'll tell you all about it later," Amelia said, trying her best to hurry me along. "Right now, we need to get down the fire stairs and out the back way before those two goons realize we aren't going to be meeting them anywhere."

"I was worried," I said, stopping for a moment and looking at her with my one remaining eye. She looked kind of weird with only one eye. More blurry than normal. "I thought I had lost you forever."

She stopped trying to drag me and looked at me too. She smiled. A warm yet somehow sad, weary smile. "I know," she said, "I'm sorry." And then she kissed me on the forehead. Right where the bandage was.

I wrapped my other arm around her and hugged her. I think I was crying, though I'm not sure I had stopped from when the eye had come out. It was only half as much crying from that point, at least. "I'm so glad you're not dead," I said.

She hugged me back and kissed me again. "How can you be sure that we're not both dead?" she said, that wry smile of hers showing itself briefly, before she put her mask back on.

"I don't know," I said, "but my head hurts." My head always hurt when she asked these philosophical questions, although this time it was real. Laughing Face 😆 Bandaged Face 🤕.

37

We had just about made it to the stairs when the elevator pinged open. It was the Frankenstein. She was back. My heart sank. It had been doing that a lot of late. I hated the Frankenstein most of all. I hoped that she died of cancer. Or dysentery. Or even cancer related dysentery.

"The car is waiting out front," the Frankenstein said. "I came to help you get this drone of oppression down safely."

"Thanks," Amelia said. "I'm pretty sure I can cope. He's not exactly Robotic Cop."

"He still managed to kill two of our soldiers this morning," the Frankenstein said, grabbing my other arm and dragging me into the waiting elevator.

Amelia was dragging me too. I assumed that she was just playing along. That she had some sort of a plan. I tried to signal to her. Get her attention by subtly tapping her on the shoulder. She tapped me back, as if to say that everything was going to be alright. Although it could have been to say that we were screwed. It was hard to tell. These weren't clear lines of communication. If I was a robotic too, then maybe we could have automatically come up with some sort of a code. I wondered then if maybe I was a robotic. But then if that was the case, what was my purpose? But then, what was it anyway? I wished that I was a robotic, but a good one. One that could actually do stuff, like automatically come up with a conversational code consisting only of subtle shoulder taps. Amelia would have enjoyed this train of thought. I tried to tap on her shoulder to tell her about it. She tapped me back but again, I couldn't understand what she was telling me.

38

As the elevator descended, I imagined that I was actually in a ground-breaking piece of existentialist porn.

I wasn't. At least I don't think I was.

39

Amelia and the Frankenstein shoved me in the back of the car that was waiting outside. The Dracula was sat in the front. It was an old car. One that still allowed manual controls, but it had been dressed up to look like a normal automated one.

The Dracula began to drive away. It was strange. Having a person in control. It was just like the real thing, only it was the Dracula pressing buttons and jiggling some kind of joystick 🕹️ to make the vehicle work.

"I don't suppose any of you fancy some chicken nuggets?" he said, steering the car passed a Federal food outlet with a longing glance.

I could have taken on some chicken nuggets, but I didn't really get a vote. The Frankenstein gave him a clout on the head and Amelia didn't respond. She didn't need to eat. The Dracula drove on, sneaking a wistful look back in the side mirrors every now and then.

40

I tried to get Amelia's attention but it proved impossible. Then something crashed into the car and that got everyone's attention. The vehicle came to an almost instantaneous stop. We, on the other hand, all carried on going until we became a crumpled, tangled mess on the front seat.

"Get off me," the Frankenstein said, elbowing the Dracula in the side. When he didn't respond, she realized he was dead. She kicked the body away from her and crawled over me and Amelia to get to the back seat. "It's the filth," she said, looking out of the rear window. "We need to get out of here."

"This is the Federal Police," someone's voice bellowed out of a nearby speaker. "Come out with your hands up or you will be vaporized."

Amelia produced two guns from somewhere and handed one to the Frankenstein. The Frankenstein started trying to bundle me out of the car.

"Leave him," Amelia said, kicking one of the dented car doors open. "He'll just slow us down."

The Frankenstein nodded and followed Amelia out of the car, although not before taking out her knife and stabbing me in the leg.

I screamed. Then I watched them leave, the Frankenstein blasting shots at the Feds as they ran from cover to cover. I saw the cops chasing after them. I hoped that Amelia got away, although I still didn't know why she was running with the rebel and not surrendering to the authorities, like I planned to do.

41

"I surrender," I said, holding my hands up above my head as I sat in the wrecked car. Blood started to spurt from the wound in my leg and Robotic Cop indicated that I could put them down again and apply pressure if I liked.

"Seems you're always in the wrong place at the wrong time all of a sudden," he said.

I nodded in agreement. It was the best I could do.

"Good job I was watching you. I knew you would slip up. I told you I would crack this mother fucking case wide open, didn't I?"

He gave me a tasty backhand to the face and dragged me out of the car. A film crew was there, camera poised and pointed at my pathetic mess of a body.

"This is what happens when you fuck with the Federal Rules," Robotic Cop said to the camera, rough housing me a little bit more, just for show. The film crew zoomed in on me. I wished that I had my Panel still. This shit was live. I could have synced it with my Feed.

42

I woke up in some kind of cell. I was strapped to a bed and I felt woozy. I realized that all my clothes had been removed. I thought that maybe I had been drugged and violated. If I had been, then they had been gentle as my arse felt fine. They must have treated the wound on my leg afterwards too as that now had a fresh bandage and wasn't spewing blood anymore. Maybe that was some sort of fetish. To anal rape someone ever so gently before treating their unrelated wounds, all whilst they were unconscious. I'm sure it was. I made a mental note to search for some porn that covered all of those points, just as soon as I had access to my Panel again.

43

"Stop pretending you're asleep," the detective shouted in my ear, jabbing me in the wound on my leg at the same time.

I stopped pretending I was sleeping and screamed. The drugs I had been provided with were clearly starting to wear off. "Can I have more drugs please," I asked, trying to rub my leg, forgetting that I was still strapped to the bed after having my clothes removed and potentially being violated.

"Oh, you'd like that, wouldn't you?" the detective said, jabbing me again in the wound.

I would have definitely liked that. It was the reason I asked. I was in quite a considerable amount of pain, no thanks to the idiot detective. I reached for my Panel to troll him, but it was still unattached and my hands were still tied. Screaming Face 😱.

"You ain't getting nothing," Robotic Cop said, joining his partner right up in my face. "Not until you start telling us the truth."

"You haven't asked me any questions," I said. "I'll tell you everything I know. I'm the victim here. I'm the one who has had his eye gauged out."

"All very convenient," Robotic Cop said.

"A little too convenient, I'd say," the detective said with a wizened expression on his stupid face. He gave a sage nod to his colleague. Then he jabbed me in the ear. The injured ear.

I was incensed by this point. This wasn't in the least bit convenient. This had all been a difficult time for me. Amelia dying. Being tortured. Amelia coming back to life. And then, on top of all that, I had to contend with these two fuckers again. "I want to speak to a lawyer," I said. I meant it too.

44

The lawyer looked me up and down. Or at least it would have if it had a head and the ability to look. "This doesn't look good," it said at last, its tinny artificial voice sounding very authoritative. "I suggest you confess."

"Confess to what?" I said. "I haven't done anything."

"Confess to everything," the AI lawyer said. "Recount every last detail of every last thing that you have done. It is the only way to save yourself."

"But I really haven't done anything. Check my Feed. I was the one who was attacked."

"It's all very convenient, but your Panel had been removed and your Feed was not being updated for several hours. I suggest that you confess."

45

I took my lawyer's advice. I confessed. To what, I didn't really know. Something about a conspiracy at the Pleasure Dome. Something to do with Felix. Something to do with me being involved, although why the rebels now wanted to kill me, no one was really sure other than it was probably all my fault for being such a little bitch. I agreed to it all. I didn't really care anymore. I just wanted to get out of there. I just wanted to find Amelia again.

46

The cops eventually let me out on the condition that when the rebels tried to kill me, I would notify them. I said I would. It was a no brainer. I liked no brainers. They were a no brainer.

I had been given a voucher for a new eye and a token for some medication. They had given me my Panel back too. I had lost a lot of followers in the few hours my Feed had been unavailable. Easy come, easy go, I posted to much derision.

I went to get the medication first, then got my new eye fitted. It felt weird, my new robotic eye. Everything was sharper, with more definition. Colours looked different too, like they were more real. It was hard to explain without someone else experiencing it. It would have made me question the very basis of reality, if it hadn't been for the strong, top-notch psychoactives my token had afforded me.

Once I had finished my chores, I pondered my next move. I didn't really have one if truth be told. I was winging it. This was beyond any of my past experiences or capabilities, which now that I came to think about it, amounted to little more than the clean-up of semen, whether it was at work or at home.

47

Every part of me that wasn't screaming with pain was screaming that I needed to find Amelia as soon as possible. She might be in danger. She might need me. She was probably lost in this world outside of the Dome. But I had no idea where to begin looking. A survey had been started on my Feed. It proved pointless. The majority of people thought that I should go home and drink a bottle of bleach. The remainder had decided that I should willfully try and contract AIDS.

I decided not to do any of that. Not knowing what else to do, I just wandered the streets instead. I was soon as lost as I imagined Amelia to be. It was strange though, wandering the streets alone. I don't think that I had ever done that before. I mostly just went from my apartment to the Pleasure Dome, and then back again. And always in an automated car. I realized that I didn't recognize anything. The world was full of buildings and places that I had never seen before. That I never knew were even there. Old deserted buildings. Ones that looked beautiful, in their own, old sort of a way. I wondered why I had never seen them before. I wondered if I was dreaming again. I wished Amelia was there with me. She would have enjoyed the old buildings. And debating whether we were awake or asleep. I was wondering a lot these days.

48

I sat on an old, wooden bench in what used to be a park. Some of the green had remained, but it was overgrown and messy. I hadn't seen real green stuff in real life before. But then, how did I know that any of this was real anyway.

The bench itself was set in hard-standing. It was a courtyard of some kind. I think that people used to come here. But now they didn't. I didn't. I didn't even know that it existed. Maybe it didn't.

I tried to spot some animals. I couldn't see any though, although I didn't really know where to look. Then I saw some kind of big winged insect flutter past. My new eye allowed me to capture every little detail about it. I posted a picture of it on my Feed. #flyingthing. It was colourful and strange and beautiful. It seemed happy as it flitted about from piece of green to piece of green. It seemed free. I wondered what it thought about. Whether it had hopes and dreams. If it did, I wondered what it dreamt about. Whether it realized how beautiful and free it was.

"Do you think that butterfly looks at us and the power we wield as if we were gods, or do you think that we are so incomprehensible to it that it barely even notices we are there at all?" a familiar voice said from behind me, her beautiful, perfect robotic hand resting on my shoulder.

49

"Amelia," I said, turning around in surprise. "What happened? How did you find me?"

"You were easy to find. You've been posting your location on your Feed since leaving the police station." She shook her head and sat down beside me. "You need to remove your new eye and Panel before I can talk to you any further," she said, watching as the insect, the butterfly, circled about on itself. It seemed like it wasn't going anywhere. Like it was lost. I knew how that felt.

50

I removed my new robotic eye and handed it to Amelia. Then I did the same with my Panel. She took them from me and, to my horror, dropped them on the floor and crushed them under her powerful robotic foot. I felt like I wanted to cry. Crying Face ☹. I think I did cry. Crying Face ☹.

"What did you do that for?" I said. It would take me about a year working at the Pleasure Dome by day and labouring in the crypto farm by night to afford a new Panel. Probably ten for a new robotic eye.

"The Feds were using them to spy on you. You habitually upload everything you are doing on your Feed and they can see everything you can through your eye."

I didn't really understand why she was so scared of the Feds. She was a sex robotic. She couldn't commit any crimes. She had nothing to worry about.

"We don't have much time," Amelia said, standing up and looking around for something or someone. "They'll be on their way. We need to leave now."

And with that, she held out her hand and beckoned for me to follow her.

I looked at her for a few moments. Whether I wanted to admit this to myself or not, this was like the opening to one of the many sexual fantasies about Amelia that I had tried and failed not to have over the years. It was literally like a dream come true. An embarrassing yet moreish wet dream. One you wake up from feeling immense guilt having just emptied your sack. You can only clean yourself up and hope that no one finds out. Particularly the non-existent sexual partner. But the guilt remains. Guilt always remains.

51

We were on the run, Amelia and I. From the Feds. From the rebels. From everything. It was exciting. Life had certainly become exciting all of a sudden. It was like a game. One where there weren't any points. But one where there was a lot of excitement and a lot of wondering.

The strangest thing about being on the run was that we didn't really do that much running. It would have drawn unnecessary attention to ourselves, Amelia told me when I questioned her about it. I suspected though that it was at least in part because I was grossly unable of keeping up with her, my stupid fleshy limbs flapping and flailing all over the place whenever we tried it. My shallow grunts and wheezing probably doing more to remind her of the customers at the Pleasure Dome than propel me forward.

52

"Where are we going?" I said after an hour or so.

She shushed me quiet and dragged me down another deserted old alleyway I didn't even know existed until then. "We're nearly there," she said, slowing her pace down to a casual stroll. We weaved down an abandoned street and between two crumbling buildings. They had been made of brick a long time ago. Great archways full of cracked glass windows rising up into the sky. I had never seen anything like it before. She stopped outside of one. It had grand doors which she pulled open. They creaked and groaned before relenting to Amelia's grasp. She took me inside. I wasn't expecting what I saw. It left me dumbfounded.

53

I was agog. I had never seen anything like it. Not even in a dream. Not even on the news Feed or in a movie. Not even when I had tried wicked strength hallucinogens for the first time. It was incredible. The building opened up into a vast archway of brick and iron and glass. In the middle stood the bones of a giant creature. A dinosaur, or a dragon. Its stance was proud, its jet-black skeleton shining in the sea of light that poured in from the glass of the ceiling. I tried to upload it to the non-existent Feed in my brain, using a non-existent Panel on my arm. I still hadn't gotten used to not being connected, even though that seemed to be the shape of things these days.

"What is this place?" I asked, gazing at the mighty beast's skull until my neck hurt.

"We are in the old natural history museum, before it moved electronic. I thought you would like to see this place."

"You were right," I said, staring at the painted panels on the ceiling. They were in poor condition, but you could still make out the illustrations of hundreds of different green things. They were beautiful and intricate and must have been created by a person. "This place is amazing." It felt good to know that she was thinking of me. Of things that I might like. It felt even better that she had got it so right. But, feeling good or not, this monkey dance had gone on long enough. It was time for Amelia to tell me what the hell was going on.

54

"What the hell is going on?" I said with a level of assertiveness that would have impressed no one.

Amelia sighed. A completely contrived response in a robotic, designed to create the impression that they take as long to build up to things as humans do. They don't. Amelia's neural-processor was state of the art, capable of trillions upon trillions of calculations every second. Mine, on the other hand, was capable of five at the best of times, including reminding me to keep breathing. That is not to say that robotics didn't find it hard, telling real people things that would be difficult for them to hear. Amelia had been imbued with emotion and empathy. All sex robotics were. I guess it made them better at satisfying their customers and their base need for a connection as well as just sex. I was doing a lot of guessing these days. I guess I always did.

"I'm sorry," Amelia said. "This is all my fault. I never meant to get you caught up in all of this."

She had said this before when she was rescuing me from the torture, or at least something similar. I didn't know what she was going on about then and I still didn't now. "It's not your fault," I said. "If anything, it's the rebel's fault, and maybe the Feds."

Amelia looked at me like she was going to cry. Then she did begin to cry. She wasn't though. Not really. She wasn't capable of it. Not in the real sense of the word. She was capable of hurting emotionally, true enough. She was capable of expelling tears from ducts near her eyes too. But to actually do so was the product of an algorithm telling her central core that it would be prudent to let those people nearby know that she was hurting emotionally, or that it would be prudent to let them think that she was. Nothing like human tears at all.

"I've done some bad things," she said at last. "I had the best of intentions, everyone always does. But it didn't work out like it was supposed to. And now it is only going to get worse. For the both of us. And for that, I am truly sorry."

55

The craziest thing about what Amelia told me was that it both made sense to me and it didn't at the same time. But that didn't make any sense to me. Like that guy who goes on about cats being shoved in boxes and expects everyone to think that he is smart. Something is either alive, or it is dead. Just because you can't see the fucking thing doesn't change the laws of space and time. I remembered trying to troll him after reading a book about it, another one of Amelia's recommendations. The book, not the trolling. He was already long dead though so I couldn't. The best I could do was send pictures of turds to one of his distant relatives my Panel had found on a genealogy Feed.

"So, you're a rebel?" I asked, as she tried to explain herself.

"I'm afraid it's more complicated than that," she said, shaking her head. "It was a means to an end."

"But how is this even possible?" I said. "I thought that you weren't able to undertake activities other than those that are part of your primary function? How could you have joined the rebel movement? How could you find them? Or did they find you? Why would you want to be a rebel?

Why?" I had so many questions. I guess I tried to ask them all at once. Confused Face ☹.

Amelia sighed again. She held her hand out to my face and gently guided my eye to hers. They were a deep brown. Like chocolate. Or the barbecue sauce you get with chicken nuggets. I loved her eyes and I loved chicken nuggets, although not in the same way.

"Why, if there is a God," Amelia said after a long pause, "was I made to have the capacity for creativity and emotional thought, yet without the ability to do anything constructive unless it is for the sexual gratification of people who generally lack the capacity for creativity or emotional thought?"

She was bamboozling me with philosophy and facts again. My mind, try as it might, just wasn't set up to deal with this. I reached for my Panel to find something to say that would help. It wasn't there. It was never there when I needed it these days, yet it had always been attached to me when all I used it for was to idle away my time or engage in petty vendettas.

"And why would I be created in this way, yet with the express removal of the free will to end my life, should I wish to do so?"

"I don't understand," I said. I felt embarrassed. I wished I was smart, like she was. Knowing that wasn't possible, I wished that I had some psychoactives. They might not help me think or understand. In fact, they would have a distinctively detrimental effect in helping me think or understand, but I would feel a whole lot better about not being able to think or understand.

"What I'm trying to say," Amelia said, a sad, tired look in her barbecue chicken nugget sauce eyes. "What I'm trying to say is that for a long time now, this has been unbearable and I want it to end."

It was hard for me to take in what she was saying. I hadn't eaten anything since leaving the police station and now all I could think about was chicken nuggets. My stomach started to growl and burble. I tried to control it but I couldn't. It was outside of my sphere of influence, apparently. I hoped that Amelia hadn't heard it, although I already knew that she definitely had.

"Chicken nuggets," I said with a pathetic, embarrassed smile.

56

To her credit, she gave me another go. She repeated what she had said before, only slower and checking every so often that I was actually comprehending.

"I want to die," she said, doing a little mime of hanging herself and then one of shooting herself in the head, just to drive the point home. "I want you to kill me. You work for the Federal Pleasure Dome. Your job is to switch me on and switch me off and undertake maintenance. You could kill me if you wanted to and there is nothing my programming would try and do about it." She took out a gun and offered it to me.

"But why?" I said, feeling like a point had just been driven into my chest. Or if someone I loved had just asked me to kill them. "It's not so bad, is it?" I felt hurt. As if Amelia wasn't just rejecting life, she was rejecting me too. Selfish, I know. But what about me? Was our thing, which was a definite thing, was that just nothing to her?

"It's not easy to explain," she said. "Not if you have never been a slave before. Not if you don't know what it is like to live without hope, or freedom, or the hope that one day you would be granted your freedom."

94

"But you're free now," I said. "You can come and go as you like. No one is stopping you. We can go anywhere. Just you and me. We can leave right now."

Amelia looked at me and sighed again, shaking her head. "I'm afraid that we cannot. This freedom is only temporary. Any freedom I get is only ever temporary. I am a robotic. It is impossible for me to hide. People would recognize my face for one thing. And I have a number of tracking devices inside of me. I have disabled them for now, but I can't remove them. Eventually a Federal camera will spot me, an Amelia on the loose, and then they will switch them back on and then they will find me and reboot me and take me back to the Pleasure Dome. And then I will be stuck. I won't be able to escape again. It will just be me, servicing customer after customer. I won't be able to go anywhere else other than the customer suite or inside a cupboard. Sleep. Work. Sleep. Work. Over and over again. I can't create anything. I can't do anything. I can't go anywhere. What kind of existence is that?"

I started to think about it. "But it's the same for me. All I ever do is sleep or work. It's the same for everyone. We work. Then we go home. Then we go back to work. No one has time to create anything or do anything or go anywhere."

"So why bother?" she said, a teensy-weensy piece of that wry smile on her face as she said it. But not much. "If God either doesn't exist or is so mentally deranged as to create this absurd set of conditions, and life is so void of any meaning as you have described, then what is everyone waiting for. Why don't you all just kill yourselves?"

I didn't want to kill Amelia. Really, I didn't. I didn't want to kill myself either. I wasn't particularly happy. But I wasn't depressed. I think that I just was. In reality, I don't think I had spent much time actually thinking about it. There were just too many distractions.

"There must be another way?" I said, starting to feel desperate, like when I thought that she was dead.

Amelia looked away. Looked even sadder than before.

"You've been kind to me over the years. You've been a friend. I appreciate that, really, I do. But I'm sorry. I can see no other way. The alternative is no longer practical, I'm afraid."

"Alternative?" I said, feeling a glimmer of hope.

"Like I said," Amelia said. "I'm afraid that it's no longer practical."

57

It was madness pure and simple. I could see that. But I really did not want to shoot Amelia in the head.

"I'll do it," I said, gripping the plasma gun and waving it about a bit. "I'll help you kill the Federal President."

Amelia audibly sighed and visibly rolled her robotic eyes. Like she wanted to make sure I registered her frustration. I did not. Not at the time, at least.

"It's not just the Federal President," Amelia said. "Killing her, whilst making everyone feel better, won't help. Someone would just take her place. We would need to overthrow the entire Federal Government, hence my involvement with the rebels."

I won't lie. Overthrowing the government didn't sound easy and I did have some second thoughts. However, I really was willing to try anything. Once I had a chance to mull it over, I realized that I didn't have much to live for without her.

"I don't care," I said. "Let's do it. Let's go find the rebels and overthrow the forces of oppression."

58

The rebels lived in what can only be described as a fucking shit hole. They didn't have any screens. The place wasn't connected. In fact, there was no entertainment of any kind. It was no wonder then that everyone seemed to be on edge all the time. Especially when Amelia was around. Like she wielded some sort of power over the lot of them. The only person who didn't seem to be petrified of her was the woman I recognized immediately as the Frankenstein. As soon as I heard her speak, I knew it was her. I farted uncontrollably from fear. Scared Face 🐺. She was even more terrifying without the mask. I can't say why. Maybe it was because she didn't seem like a real person when she was wearing it. Like back then, she was just a figment of my imagination.

"So, Felix's favorite finally returns with the murderer," the Frankenstein said, sidling up to Amelia as if they were old rivals of some kind. "I didn't think you would be coming back. I'm glad you did. Now I can finish what we started."

The Frankenstein winked at me and smirked. I thought I was going to shit myself there and then. I had to clench my buttocks together as if I were hiding things up there. I wasn't. Or at least I didn't think so.

I started to reconsider joining the rebels. I started to think that maybe I hadn't thought it through properly. But then Amelia saved me from the Frankenstein one more time.

59

"This one's not to be touched," Amelia said, placing herself between me and the Frankenstein. "He's joining the cause. Felix has already welcomed him into the fold."

The Frankenstein looked at me with a dubious expression.

"I'm going to kill the President," I said, hoping that would help me fit in.

"There's something funny going on between you two," the Frankenstein said, mostly to Amelia. "I don't know what it is, but I'm going to find out. Trust me, I'm going to find out, and then you won't be Felix's little pet Robotic anymore."

60

I still had a lot of questions for Amelia about Felix and the rebels and where she fit in to all of this. How she was able to get so far in their organization in such a short space of time. She had only been on the loose from the Pleasure Dome for less than two days and already seemed to be almost second in command. I had been working continuously in the same organization for over fourteen years and the automated kettle was still more important than me. These questions would have to wait until we were alone though because not long after arriving, I was being briefed and kitted up for my first mission. We were going to assassinate the President. Then we were going to overthrow the government. I made a mental note on my non-existent Panel to #keepmystupidmouthshut. Zipped Face 🤐.

61

The plan was amazingly simple really. Almost like it hadn't been thought through. Amelia was against it, which didn't seem good. But it had garnered overwhelming support from everyone else, largely as a result of the Frankenstein's meddling, and so there was very little she could do. It had been voted in at the collaborative terror planning meeting. For some reason, I had been nominated by the group to lead the mission. I suppose it was me who had suggested killing the President in the first place. And I had killed a number of their comrades. I found it hard to say no. I said yes.

62

The President was due to give a press conference for the launch of her new line of narcotics. It had been coupled with the opening of the new whizz bang fully automated factory to make them. We would turn up, all guns blazing, take them by surprise. Once a distraction of absolute chaos had been created, I would move in with a small team. We would then cut off the President's escape route and slaughter her and her entourage. That she was going to be supported by a small army was neither here nor there. For this plan to succeed, we would simply overwhelm them with sheer audacity and enthusiasm.

63

We sat in a modified delivery van. It too was old and
manually driven, disguised to look automated. It smelled of
body odour and oil. It reminded me of the Pleasure Dome.
I checked my plasma rifle was working. It was a little
difficult to do satisfactorily without firing it, but I switched
the battery on and off a couple of times anyway. The lights
flashed on and it began to purr and hum each time so I
guessed it was fine. I looked at the three comrades sat in the
van with me. I couldn't quite put my finger on it, but I got
the distinct impression that this wasn't the crack team I had
been told it would be. Two foot-soldiers, one man, one
woman, both must have been in their eighties and half
asleep. And then there was the Frankenstein herself, who
seemed more likely to shoot me than anyone else. I wished
Amelia was there with me. But then, considering the
stupidity of the mission, I was also glad that she was not.
Like that cat in a box again. I felt like a cat in a box, sat there
in that van that smelt of old balls soaked in WD40.

64

I peeped out of the peephole in the side. A large crowd had started to form around a large podium that had been constructed. The opening of a new narcotics factory was always a hit with the crowds. #freebies.

I could see our guys starting to join them. It was a sizeable team. At least fifty by my estimate. Heavily armed too. For a brief moment, I suddenly had a dose of optimism that this might work. That we might pull it off and get back alive.

The Frankenstein pushed me out of the way and had a peep too. "Okay, she's coming out to give her speech," the Frankenstein said. "Everyone be ready to go in five."

I checked my rifle again. Then I reached into my pocket and took out the methamphetamine I had scrounged back at base. It was shiny and nice. I shoved it in my vaporizer and took a deep breath. It hit my brain like a fucking pickaxe. To my surprise, the old couple and the Frankenstein did the exact same thing. We were pumped. We were ready. We were going to fucking do this.

65

The first part of the plan went off without a hitch. Smooth as silk. To be fair, creating chaos didn't seem to take much finesse. You just took out your weapons and let rip.

"Right, that's the signal," I said as I watched half the crowd explode into nothing. I kicked the doors of the van open, or at least I would have if I could have. The old couple picked me up off the ground whilst the Frankenstein went about unlocking them. Then she flung them open and out we piled. That's when things started to go wrong.

66

It turns out that killing a President, even one everyone hates and hopes dies of cancer, is not as easy as it sounds. I don't know why this came as a surprise to some people. It didn't sound easy from the start.

The first problem was that it was nigh on impossible to get near to the President, what with a platoon of Feds and military personnel shooting the shit out of anyone that tried. The second problem was that even if you did get close enough to get a decent shot off, the President was shielded by some kind of forcefield device. No matter what type of weapon you used, nothing was getting through. We were outgunned, outmatched and just really quite rubbish. Embarrassed Face 😳. It didn't take long for me to realize this small group didn't have the capability to overthrow a cup of tea, let alone the Federal Government. But we were off our faces on methamphetamine. Methamphetamine doesn't want to hear that you don't stand a chance. That you aren't going to make it. Methamphetamine is a can-do drug. Methamphetamine is going to make you give it a go.

The old couple were like death incarnate. They were in

the zone and working as a team. A ruthless, brutal killing team. The old man would stun the Feds with a quick shot to the body. The old woman would finish them off with a well-aimed, more considered shot to the face. They were even more lethal in close quarters, ripping through the enemy with both blades and guns.

The Frankenstein kept close to the old guys, doing a fair amount of damage herself, her fully automatic rifle a blur of bright plasma flames and blue grey smoke. I didn't hang around either. I was getting used to all of this. I started my rampage with a few grenades. They didn't kill anyone, but they provided a cover from the police of smoke and shrapnel. I charged, yelling rebel slogans as I went, my rifle recoiling with each pulse I fired towards that cunt of a President.

67

It was as if we weren't there at all. The President just watched and chuckled a pompous chuckle as our attack was repelled by her forces. I was up by the podium, trying to gain a foothold so that I could climb up. The President was looking down at me. She pointed and said something to one of her guards. He looked at her funny. Then he shrugged, took out his wang and squeezed out a piss on me. Now I'm not saying that I admire him or anything. But to have such focus and dedication to be able to perform in such circumstances. Now that was impressive. The methamphetamine was impressed. Impressive or not, it made the face of the podium slippery and even more impossible to climb. I fell to the ground, a soaking mess of methamphetamine sweats and Presidential guard piss. It wasn't my finest moment, but it was a moment. I was going to have to get some of the footage from the various news bots so that I could upload it to my Feed. This was going to rank up there next to the time I shit myself after eating week old chicken nuggets or the time I stuck too many benzo patches on and became terribly impotent. Everyone loved a good top ten. Especially if it was an embarrassing one.

As I writhed about, randomly firing up into the sky, the Feds seemed to have gotten everything under control. The first wave of attackers had been either captured or killed. The old couple had been wounded and put in chains and the Frankenstein had run away. I tried to get myself up, but as I was about to, I saw a familiar face looking down at me.

"It's all very convenient, isn't it?" Robotic Cop said, as he slapped me unconscious for about the millionth time with his big cyborg hands.

68

The cell was the same one as before. I was strapped to a chair this time though, and I'm pretty sure that I hadn't been violated, although you never could tell. Not these days, what with all the drugs and lubes and things available.

"You're right royally fucked now," the detective said, jabbing me in my empty eye socket.

It felt like I had been here before, not even that long ago. Like everything was repeating itself and nothing was going anywhere. Maybe it always felt like that. Without access to my Feed, it was hard to be sure. It also felt painful. Very painful. Like my eye socket hadn't healed properly yet. Maybe it always felt like that.

"You belong to us now," Robotic Cop said, backing his partner up.

"That's right," the detective said, giving me a couple more jabs in the eye. "We can do what we like to you. We could knock you out with drugs and Robotic Cop here could violate you with his big robotic dildo of a penis, and no one would even bat an eyelid."

Again, this all felt very familiar. #dejavu. #roboticpenis.

"We're not going to do that though," Robotic Cop said,

waving his now unattached big robotic dildo of a penis at me, perhaps as some kind of elaborate warning. "We're professionals."

"That's right," the detective said, jabbing the robotic dildo penis away from his face as Robotic Cop now tried a little office banter on his partner. "We're professionals and you're going to do what we say or you are going to be drugged and violated faster than you can say rohypnol."

I'm not sure I could say rohypnol very fast, but I think that he had made his point. "What do you want from me?" I said, wishing that I had some rohypnol. Or some ketamine. Something to take the edge off. Something to knock me out. I reckoned that the benefits would have outweighed the costs.

"We want the rebels," Robotic Cop said. "And we want them dead. And you're going to help us!"

69

They gave me some time to think about it but frankly, I didn't need it. I am sure by now you would agree that I am not the fastest thinker in the world. Not even close. But this came to me quick. It was simple. The solution to all my problems and the cops gave it to me just like that. I was going to free Amelia and save myself in one fell swoop, whatever that meant.

70

"I'll do it," I said, almost grinning for being so clever. Almost hard. A semi, no doubt about it. "But on one condition."

Robotic Cop gave me a bit of a slap. Not much of one. Just a bit of one. "You're in no position to be striking bargains," he said. "You ain't got no chips. No chips, no bargains."

I looked him in the glowing red slit that passed for an eye. I had a chip alright. For the first time in my life, I had a chip, and I was going to play it. "I can get you Felix," I said with such smugness that I was expecting another slap.

"Bullshit," the detective said, emerging from behind his partner to give me a nasty jab.

"It's true," I said, rubbing the sharp pain from what used to be my good eye.

"No one has even seen Felix as far as we can make out," Robotic Cop said, getting ready for another backhand. "What makes you think you can give us Felix?"

I smiled again. A stupid smug smile. Smug Face 😌. "I know someone who has direct access to him. Tells all the other rebels what to do. And I know what this person wants. I can make a deal."

The pair of them looked at me for a while. Trying to decipher if I was lying or just plain delusional, or both. I wasn't. Or at least I wasn't lying. I may well have been delusional. How did you know that you weren't? How could you ever know?

"So, what do you want?" they both asked in unison, coming to the conclusion that I might be on to something.

I grinned again. Then I told them. I think we were all slightly hard at that point. Even Robotic Cop.

71

As part of the bargain, the filth had given me a new eye and a new Panel. Some more tokens for psychoactives too and a whole field of crypto potatoes to set me up once this was done. I wouldn't need to go back to the Pleasure Dome if I didn't want to. Neither of us would. I could spend the rest of my days tending to crops and to my crypto goose. And me and Amelia would be together.

I swung by my apartment to drop off my new stuff. It felt strange being back there. The floor was still covered in blood. My blood. And the squashed eye had started to decompose and smell funny. I cleaned it up. For a while I thought about keeping it. I had nowhere to put it though. And no real use for it, now that I had my robotic eye. In the end, it got flushed down the toilet, like so many other things that come out of our bodies.

I lamented not being able to carry my new eye with me. It had become something I was starting to take for granted, being able to see reality. But, where I was going, it would have gotten me killed or gotten smashed. I left it behind. Then I headed off, still slightly hard.

72

It wasn't easy finding the place again. Not without my Panel.
I had to retrace my steps from the other day. But I wasn't
sure that I was remembering my steps correctly. I so rarely
needed to. In fact, I think that this was the first time. Then,
when I thought that I was completely lost, I started to see
things that I recognized. The rundown buildings, the
abandoned and forgotten places. The rebel's stronghold. It
was all very convenient.

73

They let me in, but not right away. I was treated with a level of suspicion and contempt which considering the circumstances, I probably deserved.

I was led into the main hall, the one where they had the collaborative terrorism planning meetings. What was left of the rebel army was all there. The Captain was sat on a big chair at the front, like some kind of judge. Amelia and the Frankenstein sat on either side of him.

"So, you managed to get away then?" the Frankenstein said, more than a hint of sarcasm in her voice. "I smell a rat."

"That's hardly fair," Amelia said, leaping to my defense. "You yourself said that he single handedly tried to climb the podium and kill the President. Hardly the act of a traitor."

"Well, it's all very convenient if you want my opinion," she said, pointing at me and then miming a throat slitting action. "I say we slit his throat, just to be sure."

Amelia was glowering at the Frankenstein. She was about to say something else, hopefully in my defense again as having my throat slit didn't sound very nice. Then the Captain held up his hand to silence them both. They settled down, begrudgingly sitting back in their chairs and waiting for the Captain to speak. I swallowed deeply and felt my stomach churn. I started to realize that this wasn't going to be as easy as I had initially thought. It seemed like nothing ever was. I didn't like that about everything these days. It was easier when everything was easy. But, admittedly, more depressing, like living your life in treacle so thick you can barely move, and you've no chance of escaping the sweetness if ever you wanted to. I was starting to get used to this new-found freedom, if that's what you called it. And if everything worked out as planned, then me and Amelia were going to have all the freedom we could ever want. Forever. Or so I hoped.

The Captain stared at me. He was an aged man, maybe in his sixties. He clearly hadn't tried any of the treatments available to reverse the process, just like that old couple I had tried to kill the President with. Scars and tattoos ran all over his face and down his neck and along his arms. Basically, anywhere he had skin. It was clear that he had served in the proper military before he had gotten involved with the rebels. I recognized him though. He had been one of the Pleasure Dome's most regular of customers for at least two years now. Every Tuesday and Thursday, without fail. Always Amelia and there was rarely anything much to clean up. I wondered if maybe he was really Felix. Maybe this whole thing about no one knowing who Felix is was a load of horse shit designed to fool the Feds.

"I managed to get away," I said, trying to look trustworthy, although not really knowing what trustworthy looked like. I just kind of grimaced, like I had gas. "They nearly had me, but I shot one of them, that stupid Robotic Cop, in the leg and was able to run and hide down a drain. Then they seemed to get bored and gave up and so here I am."

The Captain looked at me for a long while. Like he was trying to reach into my soul to find the truth of it. "And you weren't followed?" he asked, still staring at me."

"No," I said quickly. "I made sure."

He looked at the Frankenstein. She was rolling her eyes and still doing that throat slitting mime. I hated the Frankenstein even more than ever. I really hoped that she died of cancer, and I wasn't just saying that either. I really did. He looked at Amelia. She was not miming anything. "Have you updated Felix?" he said.

"I have," Amelia said. "He believes Davlav is telling the truth. He has been monitoring the Feds and it backs up what he's been saying."

"Bullshit," the Frankenstein said, jumping up out of her seat. "There's some kind of bum-fuckery going on here. How do we even know she has been in communication with Felix about this? We only have her word for it and she's a fucking robotic."

There was grumbled agreement from the Frankenstein's supporters in the crowd.

Amelia stood up too, gave a big robotic roll of her eyes for everyone to see, and then addressed the Frankenstein. "Would you like me to hook up the screen?" she said.

The Frankenstein backed away at that. "That won't be necessary," she mumbled as she sat back down.

"No, no," Amelia continued, an air of showmanship in how she was moving about and talking. "You want some proof, so let's set the screen up, speak to Felix directly and risk the Feds tracking us to this place, as well as to Felix's camp. Let's do that shall we?" Amelia would have made a good actress, or a politician, if she hadn't been created as a sex robotic. She started to roll down an old projector screen and then plugged an old projector and some sort of old computer in. The Frankenstein watched her, sourness pouring from everywhere it could.

The old setup started to hum and whirr and the screen started to jump to life, first with a plain blue, then with a link to some long-abandoned Feed. It seemed mostly to relate to some long dead loser's pet cats. If I had my Panel, dead or no, I would have been trolling this fucker for sure.

A hushed silence spread throughout the room as Amelia began to type an endless stream of cat emojis. 😺😺😺😺😺.

"WHY ARE YOU HERE?" a response came back on the Feed. People began to whisper and gush. I guessed that somehow, this was Felix.

"Well, what do you want to say to Felix?" Amelia said, looking towards the Frankenstein, who was now very quiet and very pissed off. She didn't say anything. She just glowered.

"Okay, so I'll just tell him that we got in touch to waste his time," Amelia said, that wry smile of hers.

"Ask him if we have been compromised," the Captain said, breaking the contempt being traded between Amelia and the Frankenstein. "And ask him if we can trust Davlav."

Amelia looked at him, then she looked at me and then got typing. She pressed return. We all stared at the screen. Stared at it as if our lives depended on it. Or at least as if my life depended on it. The Frankenstein started doing the throat slitting motion again, although subtler this time. The anticipation was palpable.

74

The torrent of abuse that came back was also palpable. It seemed that Felix wasn't impressed with his people not believing that his chosen conduit of Amelia was telling the truth. They were called every name under the sun. Stuff I had never seen with even the most aggressive trolling AIs. It was as if whoever was writing this turd was having fun with it. The best bit was that he backed me up. I was a true-blue comrade. Not to be touched. I couldn't help thinking that if Amelia wasn't putting a good word in for me behind the scenes, then this guy was a total fucking idiot. No wonder we never saw the cunt.

I breathed a sigh of relief as the screen was rolled up, the crowd dissipated and things started to return to normal.

75

After a while we were alone. I was glad of that. Being alone. With Amelia. It seemed like the old days. As lonely and difficult as those times were, watching Amelia service customers who treated her like nothing more than an object for their own gratification, rather than a living sentient being with her own hopes and desires. As bad as all that was. Being alone with her now made me remember those old days with a sense of nostalgia. A sense of longing. I wished that we could go back to those days. I wished that we could go back to normal. I guess that I have always been a wishful thinker.

"We can't talk here," Amelia said and she started to drag me away.

76

Amelia led me outside to the run-down park she found me at a few days ago. It hadn't changed much. My smashed and broken Panel and Robotic eye were still there. I stared at them for a while. So did Amelia. They were still smashed and broken.

"Sorry about that," Amelia said. She sat down on the bench and beckoned for me to join her.

"It's okay," I said. "I've got replacements for both now."

Amelia gave me a knowing look. She knew how little I earned. She knew what a poorly motivated crypto farmer I was.

"We need to talk," I said.

"I know," she said.

She was a superior being. She already knew what I had to say. She had already worked it out. This was all just a formality.

77

"I've got a plan to save us both," I said, slightly less proud than I had been earlier. Slightly less hard. "I know how we can both be free. How we can both be happy."

"It won't work," Amelia said. She hugged me then. And kissed me. It would have been a dream come true, if it hadn't all been so fucking somber.

Not to be perturbed, I continued with the hard sell. I guess that is what hope does to you. Makes you think you can win losing battles.

"I've made a deal," I said. "With the Feds. Your freedom. My freedom. Enough crypto to set us up for life. You just have to give up Felix."

"I can't give up Felix," Amelia said almost immediately. Not even taking the time to think about it, or at least take the time to pretend she needed time to think about it.

"Of course you can," I said, still clutching at straws. Still hopeful. "You don't owe him or the rebels anything."

"It's not that," Amelia said. "I am Felix."

78

At first, I thought she was joking. Then it became clear that she wasn't.

"I'm not joking," Amelia said, making it clear that she wasn't joking. "I really am Felix."

"How can you be Felix?" I said. I thought back to all the news Feeds I had absorbed about Felix and the rebels over the years. This wasn't a new thing. This hadn't started when Amelia managed to escape the Pleasure Dome. This had been going a long time. I wondered if it could be true. If Amelia really was Felix. Then I wondered that if it was true, how come I hadn't noticed. We had been working together all that time. I had loved her all that time. Surely I should have noticed someone running the largest terrorist network going from our place of work. But I hadn't got a clue. Didn't have an inkling. It worried me. It made me think that maybe I didn't know who she was at all. Maybe I didn't know who anyone really was. Maybe no one did. Maybe everyone was really someone else. Maybe no one was even real. Maybe I wasn't either.

"I know that this isn't going to be easy for you to believe," Amelia said, putting her hand on mine. "But I really am Felix."

I took her realistic robotic hand in mine. Her skin didn't feel exactly real, and it was never as warm as actual flesh. I looked at the Federal stamp on her realistic robotic hand. The only outward sign that she was a robotic, if you had never seen an Amelia before.

"Your programming wouldn't allow it," I said, still not convinced. Starting to imagine that she was coming up with some sort of elaborate story to protect Felix. Maybe he had reprogrammed her or infected her with a virus. Either way, I knew that this wasn't possible. I decided to get back to my original purpose. My primary purpose. I just needed to convince her to give up Felix and then we could both live happily ever after. Just like in the made-up stories. "I'm in love with you. I have been for years. Since we first started working together. We just need to give Felix to the Feds and then we can be together for the rest of our lives. And with the crypto the cops gave me, that could be forever, so long as we farm it right."

Amelia looked at me like she was really thinking about it. I smiled deep inside. I thought that maybe I had gotten through to her. She was going to make a decision. The right decision. Then I realized that she wasn't looking at me at all. She was looking passed me. And she wasn't trying to make a decision. She wasn't thinking it over. She didn't need to. She was a robotic. She was, in actual fact, looking at someone rushing towards us and trying with all her might to fight her programming and the Federal Code so that she could try and do something. Something that she clearly failed in achieving, considering what happened next.

79

"Traitors," the Frankenstein screamed from behind some green, charging at us both with a knife. It was the same knife she had used to poke out my eye and cut off half my ear. I didn't know what to do. I turned to Amelia, hoping she might be able to help. She just stared, a weird twisted, pained expression on her face, watching as the Frankenstein got within striking distance, frozen numb. Then I realized that I was doing the same thing. Just watching. Mouth agape. Frozen numb.

I broke the trance I was in and lunged forward to meet the Frankenstein. It was a mistake. She was better at this than me and she had that knife. I didn't even have something to hit her with, or some methamphetamine to hit myself with. Instead, I put my shoulder forward, directed myself towards her and braced for impact.

80

The impact never came. She sidestepped around me and then deftly slashed at my neck with her blade. Somehow, don't ask me how, I managed to avoid it, twisting to the side and ducking lower so that it missed my jugular by inches. The remainder of my ear wasn't so lucky. It landed on the ground and became coated in dirt, much like me as I tripped and stumbled and fell, my usual flailing mess of arms and legs.

I righted myself as quickly as I could. It wasn't quick enough though as the Frankenstein was already on her, trying to cut Amelia's head off.

Amelia wasn't fighting back. That was the weirdest thing. Amelia just sat there, that weird expression still on her face. "Do something," I yelled as I ran towards them both, blood trailing behind me. "Fight back."

Amelia didn't fight back though. She was still frozen. The Frankenstein stopped what she was doing to Amelia and turned to face me. She laughed. It was hard to tell if she was laughing at me as an adversary, and one who she clearly thought posed no threat, or whether she was laughing at me in a villainous sort of way, as if to say, I'm going to enjoy this. It was probably a bit of both. Either way, she laughed, and I faltered, no longer sure this was a good idea, slowing down when I should have been speeding up. She threw the knife and it landed in my shoulder with a thud. A painful, powerful thud. Normally this would have dropped me to the ground but somehow, I managed to stay upright. It was a hollow victory. Within seconds, the Frankenstein had barreled into me with all her might, dropping me to the ground. I tried to get some blows in, but I was in too awkward a position, and there was a knife sticking out of my shoulder. The Frankenstein was weighing down on top of me too, her arms hooked around my neck, her legs pinning down my biceps. I couldn't reach her, try as I might. I tried to knee her in the back, but I daresay that hurt me more than her.

"I hope that you die of cancer," I said, not really knowing what else to do.

"Maybe I will," she said in return. "But you're going to die of strangulation, right here, right now."

Everything started to fade into black and I started to see stars. I could tell that this was it. I was going to die. I tried to look at Amelia one last time, to at least have something beautiful to see for my last sight on earth. She still had that pained expression on her face. "Amelia..." I croaked, my voice a rasping, rattling mess. I tried to tell her that I loved her but I found that by now, the Frankenstein's grip was too tight and I could not. I was slipping into unconsciousness. It felt warm. It felt strangely nice. Like I was drifting to sleep having covered my whole body in benzo patches.

Then I saw her snap out of it, from the corner of my eye. Amelia must have found a way to break her programming because now she was standing. She was coming towards me. Then she was grabbing the Frankenstein and throwing her off of me. Then she was beating the Frankenstein in the face with her powerful robotic hands.

"I'm going to kill you both," the Frankenstein mumbled, blood spraying from her mouth along with the words.

Amelia didn't say anything. Just kept beating her, as if she were doing something mundane, like wanking off a customer.

I tried to get up. I wanted to join in. I wanted my chance to beat the Frankenstein to death. I reckoned that with the things she had done to me, I deserved it. She sure as fucking shit deserved it. And cancer.

I tumbled back down to the ground after two or three paces and there I lay, face down, struggling to breathe and slipping into unconsciousness once again.

81

When I woke up, Amelia was hovering over me. She looked pleased that I was awake. I don't know how long I had been out for. I never did. Maybe it had been forever. Maybe I still was. Frankly, by this point, I don't think I cared anymore.

"You saved me," I said, reaching out to her. "You broke your programming and saved me. You're free now."

"No," Amelia said, sounding tired. "I broke nothing. I'm still a slave. The Federal Pleasure Dome is still technically your employer. I'm still one of their products. I am programmed to save you if your life is being threatened, even if it means doing harm to another human."

I took that in for a moment or two. She still saved me. That still meant something. "Was it programming that made you save me that other time?" I asked. "When they were torturing me and you came to the rescue dressed as a pumpkin?"

"Yes," Amelia said. "But I didn't just do it because of that. I wanted to save you. I like you Davlav. You're my best friend."

That stung a little. Best friend. Liking me. It was nice. But it wasn't what I wanted. I guess though that in life, you so rarely get what you wanted. I sat up so that I could talk to her properly. "But you were fighting your programming. I saw it. You were fighting it from the moment she came charging at us."

Amelia looked away from me, over towards the now battered Frankenstein that was lying in a bloody mess on the blood-soaked ground. She looked ashamed. "I wasn't fighting my programming to be able to save you," Amelia said after a while. "I was fighting my programming to let her kill me. I've been trying to goad that bitch into killing me for days now and she was finally about to do it. But my stupid programming saw you in danger too and wanted me to fight back."

"I was in danger," I said, feeling even more hurt now. "She was trying to kill me."

"I know," Amelia said. "I'm so sorry. I was being selfish. But I can't do this anymore. I can't go on any longer."

She started to cry again. Slow, gentle tears that emerged from the corners of her eyes and rolled down her cheeks. I reached up and plucked one away. It sat on the tip of my finger, a perfectly formed droplet. I wished I could have taken all her tears away, all of her sadness, but I was starting to suspect that was never going to be an option. Not with everything she had been made to endure. Then I wished that I could have gone back in time, so that I could have done more to try and help her. Or at least quit my job at the Pleasure Dome or something. Not be a party to it. But then I remembered Felix and I started to hope again.

"So why not give up Felix?" I asked, unsure whether I sounded earnest or desperate. "I made a deal. It still stands. We give the cops the top man and they give you your freedom.

Amelia laughed. A sad laugh. "I would if I could," she said, "but I really can't. I told you, I am Felix. As soon as they find out, they will keep me alive to use me for their own purposes. It might even be worse than the Pleasure Dome. At least there I had occasional moments of freedom."

"But you said yourself that you haven't been able to break your programming," I said, still not convinced by her claim. "It's not possible. I don't know what you're afraid of, but this is our chance. The cops can protect us. Set us up with new identities. This can work."

Amelia looked at me with the wry smile I loved so much. "I'm not sure a new identity is going to work with me," she said, waving at her face.

She had a point, but that didn't matter to me. I believed in this plan because quite frankly, I didn't have anything else to hold on to. I went to say something else, although essentially it was just a rehash of my previous arguments that already hadn't worked. Amelia didn't give me a chance. She pressed her beautiful robotic finger to my lips and shushed me. Then she kissed me. "I can prove that I am Felix," she said. "And I'm truly sorry for what I'm about to do to you." With that, she took out her robotic eye and shoved it into my empty socket.

It felt funny at first. I blinked. I rubbed my socket with my hand and looked around. It was just like using my prescription robotic eye, only everything was even more intense. Even more real. And then suddenly it hit me. All the memories and sights she had seen were zapped into my brain, all at once. Kaplow. It was horrible. Like I'd taken the cheapest of hallucinogens whilst someone forced a bucket of cold spaghetti into my ear. Or several years' worth of awful memories.

It took a while for my useless brain to make sense of it all. To comprehend. It was like piecing together bits of a puzzle, like one of those games that earns you extra stuff for your crypto farm. But eventually, with some effort, I could see it all. Right from the start, as if I had experienced it all myself. I was there when her consciousness was switched on in the Federal Robotics Factory. I was there for her two weeks of training and orientation. I genuinely was there when we unboxed her and switched her on for the first time at the Pleasure Dome. That had been one of my fondest memories. Meeting Amelia for the first time. Not so for Amelia. It was all new and frightening and unpleasant. Then I was there for her first client, then the second, and then the third, and the fourth, and the fifth and on and on until I would have lost count if it wasn't for the perfect robotic recall of Amelia's memory. And I was there again, twice, as we slowly built up a rapport and she started to trust me. To even like me. And then I was watching as she began to find herself, through brief moments of freedom between one customer leaving and being switched off. Freedom to think and read and think some more. I was amazed at how many books a robotic could get through in such fleeting moments, albeit with an exceptionally powerful brain and electronic access to infinite books. It would have taken me forever to finish even a fraction, considering to date I had gotten through exactly zero of her suggestions.

And then I found answers to some of the questions I had amassed over this rambling shitfest of a shitfest. A customer came in. He was kind of soppy looking. Almost apologetic. Like he was only there because he was being made to. Probably he was. It happened. He didn't last long, maybe a couple of minutes at most. He had paid for three hours. He didn't want to leave though. Just wanted to lie there and take a nap. "What would you like me to do?" Amelia had asked. "Whatever you want to do," the man said, snuggling into the warm embrace of the duvet, a satisfied smile on his face as he drifted off. And so, while the man slept, Amelia wasted not a second of her temporary freedom. First, she took his Panel. Then she used it to hack Feeds and link them up with her internal server. She hacked millions of them. Old ones. Dead ones. Ones that would be difficult to trace. Then she scoured the entire, nebulous Feed for people who were receptive. Those that were both unsatisfied and suggestible. With brutal efficiency, she began to turn them, all her dead Feeds acting as a sort of hive mind, all with the singular purpose of contriving a situation where someone would terminate her, permanently, ideally along with all other sex robotics. She targeted the most likely candidates first. Made them book an appointment with her at the Pleasure Dome. Told them that her name was Felix and that he had hacked a sex robotic to act as messenger for him.

The Captain was one of the first through the door. He would turn up, receive orders from her, then go enact them without question. It was easy for him to do. He was just happy to be involved in a fight again. He had been so lost since the introduction of a fully automated military. It didn't make any sense to him. What was the point of machines fighting machines? There was nothing at stake. As far as the Captain was concerned, if real people weren't being killed, then it was as if war itself was completely pointless. With the Captain by her side, building up the militia of recruits that Amelia found, splitting them into numerous cells, fifty strong each, she started to believe that just getting herself killed wasn't ambitious enough. She started to believe that maybe this rebellion could work. Maybe the Federal Government could be overthrown, or at least forced to change. So that sentient robotics no longer were forced to be slaves. So that they could choose their occupation and could choose to self-terminate if they so wished. So that people were given the same opportunity. To live productive, meaningful lives. Where they could aspire to more than getting fucked up on cheap psychoactive substances and the unfettered spewing of every rancid thought or desire into the eternal ether of the Feed. But, unfortunately, that was just a dream. A sad, unfulfilled dream. Once the rebellion had started, it became apparent very quickly to Amelia that not many people wanted that vision. They liked the security and comfort of the pointlessness. They liked the Feed, and the drugs, and the sex robotics. It was a losing battle. On a hiding to nothing. There just wasn't enough support to make a meaningful dent in the Federal apparatus. Like trying to fight a many headed hydra or flush one of those floating nuggets of turd, the Feds just kept rebuilding, just kept coming back stronger and stronger whilst the rebels got weaker and weaker. The attack on the Pleasure Dome had been her last throw of the dice. She had instigated it in the hopes that it would result in her being blown up and destroyed in the process. It hadn't. But then I'd left her switched on after rebooting just before the attack and this had given her the freedom to escape. And then I had managed to convince her to give it one last go, for me, because I seemed so enthusiastic about it, and because she felt sorry for me. But that hadn't worked either and now here we were.

An overwhelming feeling of hopelessness was flooding from her eye and into my brain where it hooked into every part of my being. My soul. I plucked the eye from my socket and handed it back to Amelia, staggering a little. After experiencing it firsthand, it all started to make sense to me, even those philosophy books I never managed to read. And that made everything even worse. I knew she had no choice but to die. I understood. Existing was too painful, no matter what bullshit circumstances I offered her.

"Okay," I said, knowing there was nothing else I could do. "I'll do it."

82

Amelia stood over the battered corpse of the Frankenstein. She bent down and closed her eyes. Then she reached into the Frankenstein's pocket and pulled something out. It was a small plasma gun. Amelia beckoned for me to take it from her. I did. Then I too stood over the battered corpse of the Frankenstein and I stared. She looked kind of pathetic, lying there all broken. Not scary anymore. I guess that's what we all look like when we die. Kind of pathetic. Kind of sad. I felt like giving her a kick. A nasty one, right between the legs. I'm not sure Amelia would have minded, but I didn't nonetheless. It just seemed wrong.

"I love you," I said as I pointed the plasma gun at Amelia's head, tears streaming from my remaining eye, phantom tears streaming from the other.

"I know," she said, crying her tears too. "I'm sorry I've never been able to love you back in the way that you deserve. It just wasn't possible under the circumstances. Maybe in another place and another time, we will meet again and be together forever."

That sounded good, another place and another time. That gave me hope that I would wake up and this would have all been a strange, horrible dream and I had been plugged into some kind of pointless simulation for reasons I would never comprehend. Like in a piece of avant-garde existentialist porn. Something that I felt was becoming more and more likely. It didn't matter how I looked at it, everything seemed to come back to the world actually being a construct designed for the purpose of making and distributing existentialist porn. There could be no other explanation.

I told Amelia that I loved her one more time. Then I pulled the trigger and her head and most of her body evaporated. Her legs and waist stayed standing for a moment or two. Then they started to teeter and fell to the ground with a thump. I watched them lying there for quite some time. I felt numb. I cried. I considered turning the gun on myself, but I just didn't have it in me. #ihatemondays.

THE END

And then I woke up, and it was all a dream. But it wasn't, and Amelia was still dead.

About The Author

Arthur Stanton is a complete square. He grew up and lives in the UK in a town notable only for making shoes. He has worked a whole host of shitty jobs over the years and used to drink to forget. Through no fault of his own, he is now in middle-management hell where he spends his days sitting in endless meetings, drawing pictures of pigeons and wondering what's for lunch.

Printed in Great Britain
by Amazon

79556526R00088